S0-BGP-103

They called her the singing nun ...

A lovely young girl with a rare gift
of song, and an even rarer gift for
bringing happiness to others, she was
a girl in love with life. And there
was a young man who very much wanted
to make her his own.

Then she met Father Clementi, who saw the
love of God and the great power of faith
in her music. And Father Clementi knew
that this young girl whom they called
"the singing nun" must dedicate herself
to a different and greater life . . .

The Singing Nun

by John Furia, Jr.

POPULAR LIBRARY · NEW YORK

All POPULAR LIBRARY books are carefully selected by the POPULAR LIBRARY Editorial Board and represent titles by the world's greatest authors.

POPULAR LIBRARY EDITION

Copyright ©, 1966, Metro-Goldwyn-Mayer Inc.

Cover photo ©, 1966, Metro-Goldwyn-Mayer Inc.

PRINTED IN THE UNITED STATES OF AMERICA
All Rights Reserved

Dedication:

**FOR MOTHER AND DAD,
WHO GAVE ME GUITARS.**

THE SINGING NUN

CHAPTER I

Even with cap and veil and her full white robes, she
seemed very small: more like a motor scooter with a
white sail billowing than a nun. Sister Ann was bent over
the handle, devoted to the business at hand, ignoring the
blare her machine made in the quiet Belgian countryside.
It was a fine day for a ride. Her small black valise was
securely tied to the rack; the guitar was well protected in
its case, and she ignored the bumps and the ruts and proceeded at full speed. She resisted the impulse to cry out
"Wheeee!" and hummed a little song to herself.

Forget any image of nuns as oversized children piously
greeting a rose colored world; triumphant over fairy tale
villains; beseeching and receiving "Divine Intervention"
in everything from preventing a roast from burning to
warming the heart of some crusty old curmudgeon. That
image is about as modern and as applicable to Sister Ann
as those instructions in ancient religious manuscripts that
". . . the Brethren . . . must not wear daggers to bed
lest in turning they impale themselves" . . . or that it is
. . . "a grave fault . . . to shoot the abbott!"

9

What is a nun? What kind of woman sacrifices things most people prize, dresses in peculiar medieval robes and immerses herself in religion? The key to Sister Ann can be found in old Dominican chronicles. They relate of the founder of their order, St. Dominic, that "it was necessary that he who loves God so much should love men dearly."

Sister Ann hummed because she was happy thinking of the new responsibilities she was taking on.

"Sister," the Prioress had told her as she was about to leave Bornham, "Your assignment at Samaritan House is going to be very different from anything you experienced here at the convent."

She loved Bornham: different or not, she would miss it . . . but she was not about to miss something coming in the opposite direction. Sentinel trees along both sides of the country lane obscured her view of the next curve. She couldn't see or hear the old peasant farmer pedalling his bicycle undeviatingly down the very center of the lane. Nor could he see her.

She was picturing Bornham, remembering the serene and stately look as she passed through its doors for the first time two years ago. No more would she hear the convent bell peeling from the high tower. No longer could she walk in the quiet convent orchards knowing the serenity of prayer and the pleasure of blossoming trees at the same time. But no more classes in the "History of the Dominican Order—13th Century," either. She smiled. God is good. She leaned to the right, into the curve.

Behind her, along the canal that ran roughly parallel to the road, an ancient towboat towed a garbage scow. It wasn't a very exciting occupation, garbage scow towing, and the Captain had fallen into the habit of calling the attention of his children who lived with him to every passing sight of any interest . . . except pretty young girls in the springtime: those sights he enjoyed in solitude. But a nun tootling along on her scooter was worth a look. He summoned the family and gave a long yank on the whistle cord.

Approaching the bend in the road at the canal from the opposite direction, the old farmer drew heavily on his pipe. "Can't hear yourself think anymore," he grumbled to himself.

Sister Ann was aroused from her reverie by the mournful whistle. Grinning, she squeezed her scooter horn in response. Then almost in her ear came the ring of a bicycle bell. She whirled and looked straight into the determined eyes of the old farmer, set on a collision course as each of them rounded the curve.

Only a few feet apart Sister Ann yanked her scooter to one side of the narrow lane, but the farmer did precisely the same. Each feinted to the right, then to the left, to avoid a collision. Unfortunately, both wound up smack in the center of the road. Confronted with imminent disaster, Sister Ann at the last moment threw her scooter to one side and skidded on the soft shoulder of the road. She did a nice somersault, winding up a tangle of white robes and scooter in a pile of dead leaves.

Sister Ann sat up, dazed but unhurt, shaking her head to clear it, and brushing leaves from her habit with a rueful smile. The flustered old farmer ran to her muttering about the right of way. What he saw was just what he suspected: one of those new young nuns. Nuns in his opinion belonged in convents the way prisoners belonged in jail and the insane belonged in asylums. Each in its proper place.

The family on the barge strained to see the disappearing Sister Ann and the old farmer as the tug took them around the bend in the canal. The children were disappointed: the picture had great promise.

Sister Ann stood up. No bones broken. Hardly a bruise. The old farmer bent and looked her squarely in the eye.

"It's a miracle we're not killed. Couldn't you see me, Sister."

"Didn't you hear my horn?"

"I had the right of way." The farmer waggled a thick finger in her face. "In plain sight, Sister! Right in the center of the road I came. Right in the center. You couldn't miss me!"

"I almost didn't!"

"What's the world coming to. A man rides down a road minding his own business and . . . boom! Out of nowhere a mad woman! A nun! Tooting a horn and looking not where she's going but where she's been!"

Sister Ann shook her arms and a leaf floated out of the full sleeves. A giggle bubbled up inside her. The thought of herself smudged, dusty, unharmed but wrapped around a motor scooter seemed to call not for handwringing but laughter.

The farmer was suddenly wary. These nuns. He expected her to pray. He himself would have cursed. But laughter?

"You're sure you are all right?"

Sister Ann righted the scooter and checked her belongings. The suitcase was still in place but her guitar had come loose. She picked it up and tried to repack it.

"The trouble with following the straight and narrow path in life," she answered, "is that it's too straight and too narrow to meet someone following the same path in the opposite direction!"

The farmer stared at her. Too bad! He couldn't quite make up his mind if the fall had addled her brain or if this was one of those typically nunlike things that you are supposed to nod your head wisely at and say: "Yes, sister," "That's so true, sister." He nodded his head, wisely.

Sister Ann gave up trying to find a place for the guitar and slung the case by its strap over her shoulder. The farmer stared at her.

"You're going on? You're going to ride that thing some more?"

"Yes."

"Down this same road?"

"Yes."

He sighed. There just didn't seem to be any reasoning with nuns. "What kind of nuns are they making in that convent, anyway?"

Sister Ann settled herself on the scooter and smiled at him. She revved the engine and waved.

"Hard headed ones, thank God!" And off she went down the road.

The old peasant stood shaking his head, wincing at the noise and the dust she raised. He looked up to the heavens, spread his hands wide and turned the palms upward in a mighty shrug. The good Lord works in mysterious ways.

There was nothing mysterious in the way He had worked with Sister Ann. She was born in the chaos of war and nurtured in its tragedy, but even as a child there was joy in her life. For many, the shattering experiences of wartime France were like pulling the opposite ends of a rubber band too taut; they snapped. When she had received the news of her father's death in an air raid, it came from the mouth of a man who also brought a legacy from her father: his guitar. It was typical of her that she had something joyous to remember of her past and her parents, rather than something sad.

She grew up in postwar France an orphan. The Brussels Conservatory of Music seemed a natural goal.

She was impressed with the city's magnificent central square; buildings almost untouched since medieval times. She was impatient with some of her studies, amused by some of her fellow students, and wore calluses on her fingers practicing the intricate variations of classical and folk guitar. Nothing mysterious there.

But she was impressed with the buildings because intuitively she knew that people could not be appreciated or fully understood apart from their surroundings. A certain pompous professor of musicology would never forget her impatience with his course. She had filled in her exam paper at the end of the first semester in a most unique way. There was but one question: "Analyze what you have learned about the relationship between mathematics and the works of Mozart—give examples."

On each page of her exam paper she had filled in the following in a neat fine script:

"Mozart's work is art. It should be enjoyed, not analyzed. If you need examples sing, play or listen to some."

She was, at the age of 23, straightforward, very attractive, gregarious, a young woman whose *joie de vivre* and warmth gave her conversation a sparkle that was endearing and imparted to her music a gossamer spell. She liked people: boys and girls, adults and children . . . even some of the professors . . . perhaps because she believed that life, like music, was meant to be enjoyed.

There was no mystery to her; so little in fact that some of her classmates laughed when they learned she had gone off to the convent at Bornham.

They reckoned without her vocation. Sister Ann was at peace in the convent. Her vocation consisted in this: although she had a warm, girlish love of mankind she had a total commitment to God. She understood commitment: she knew many who were devoted entirely to their music; she knew others who were dedicated Communists; others who believed in no more than wringing every drop of enjoyment out of life for themselves. For her commitment was simple: why not put first things first and live your life for God?

Her years at Bornham passed swiftly. She found herself a newly professed nun, her spiritual formation completed, her vows taken, standing at the threshold of a new life with a bride's radiance and a new mother's contentment. But her superiors at the convent knew there was more to being a nun than that, even if Sister Ann did not.

What finally convinced them to assign her to Samaritan House, an experimental new convent near Antwerp, was that same guitar which they had noticed when she entered the convent. Samaritan House was a very difficult assignment, particularly for a new young nun. It would be a drab and difficult life. What better nun could they send, than one who constantly exhibited happiness and joy in the songs that she composed and sang?

The scooter with its small nun came over a hill and stopped. In the distance she could see the city of Antwerp. Large buildings; a busy road; chimneys from an industrial complex writing in dirty smoke across the horizon. By the time she made her way down into the heart of the city itself, all thoughts were dispelled of Samaritan House as a fine old convent in a neighborhood of happy laughing children who would be suffered to come unto her; of hard-working mothers confiding their latest family tales; and respectful fathers tipping their hats and firmly ordering little daughters to "curtsy to Sister now." This was a rough place in a big industrial city. Littered bricks on the roadway made an obstacle course for her scooter. On the opposite side of the street were crowded buildings, eroded like the spirit of the people who lived there.

The address said Rue St. Helene. The street was cobbled and as she rounded the corner she had to slow the scooter to prevent the stones from tearing chunks out of her tires. She surveyed the buildings on either side of her, drab and soiled with the fingermarks of poverty. There was little traffic; a few workmen wearily trudged home with barely a glance at her. But she was noticed.

An emaciated woman with a perpetual frown on her face hung laundry on a makeshift line at her window. It was clean now but she knew it would be gray with soot before it was dry. A group of boys from 10 to 14 leaned against a dirty wall, smoking and staring. A nun was bad enough; a nun on a scooter was funny; a nun on a scooter almost obscured by the guitar strapped to her back was an irresistible butt of jokes.

She had to detour at one spot where a horse drawn cart, with two men loading a few pieces of battered furniture from a pile evicted onto the sidewalk, blocked her way. The mother and children waited at the curb stoically watching their furniture, far more interested in their empty future than even the amusing sight of this nun.

Further along, outside a cheap cafe, men huddled in idle knots, two or three of them tossing pieces of a shattered brick at an empty wine bottle in the gutter: their afternoon diversion.

Worse than she thought. Much.

Then she saw it. What caught her eye was the small cross at the top of the two story building. The walls were grimy; the lower portions had been used as slates for the vulgar ABC's of neighborhood children. The cross at the top began her smile. It widened as she saw the marked contrast, the stoop freshly scrubbed, the double doors newly varnished: evidence of the determination of new occupants.

Hanging beside the door was an old fashioned brass bell pull, also shining. A new, hand lettered wooden sign installed over the entrance proclaimed this to be SAMARITAN HOUSE.

Home.

CHAPTER II

The Chapel in Samaritan House was a tiny room. Whitewashed walls, scrubbed wooden floor, the altar modern in its simplicity and spartan; a long low table with two candles on it and a lacework altar cloth. Four Dominican nuns knelt there informally praying and meditating. Dimly, through her meditation on what had brought her here to Samaritan House, Mother Prioress heard the ringing of the brass doorbell. She had heard and read often that in moments of crisis the events of your life pass before you like a documentary film, in an instant of time. It hadn't happened that way to her. When the doorbell sounded in the mission compound in the Congo three years before she knew it was a warning. The sound of guns outside testified to that. But she was too busy to meditate upon her past life. Much too busy trying to help the older nuns to escape. Now, only three years after it had happened, time had softened the sharpness of pain and blurred the terrifying images. But she could still remember sweaty African faces charging with raised clubs. She could remember white men and native police firing pistols and shotguns into the enraged mob at a distance of ten feet, so close that she could see the pellets of lead tearing flesh. Time had not dulled the memory of the flames dancing up the walls of the mission compound in counterpoint to the bobbing and jumping of the fleeing mission staff. Nothing could ever erase the sight of a beloved sister eviscerated with a single blow of a native *panga*. Her meditations had been haunted for a long time by the waste of a hospital, representing years of labor, burning while scores of tribesmen roasted two priests in its flames on a wooden spit. And she could remember peering from a precarious hiding place in a fetid mound of garbage, for a final glimpse of the mission compound; the chapel gutted by fire, its crucifix dangling at a grotesque angle above where once an altar had stood. But she had managed to escape.

For six weeks she made her way alone to the safety of a port. Her tears were not tears of self pity. Nor even for the sisters and priests she knew and loved. Her tears were for people so anguished and tormented they could only find release in brutality and senseless violence. When she arrived at the Mother House in France she had only one question: when may I go back?

Mother Superior denied every such request. There had been 94 nuns from the Dominican Order in the Congo. Five French sisters returned to their convent near Paris. Seven German sisters had been flown back to Bavaria. Fifteen others were reassigned in Africa, and about 3 dozen were still at the convent and big hospital in Stanleyville. The others, including all her Belgian companions, lay in shallow ditches or crude graves.

Sister Claire had wandered through the Mother House for many months. That was what it meant to be an Apostle. That was all she had achieved in her mission work. Sixteen years ago she had left the Mother House filled with enthusiasm, determined to succeed. And she had failed.

After a time she stopped brooding on the past and began to consider the future. New methods had to be found to replace those so forcefully destroyed or shown to be unenduring in the face of chaos. A year ago her own concern with the Congo had coincided with the concern of a young, vigorous Dominican priest with a spiritually bereft parish in Antwerp.

Father Clementi's parish was a slum. Years ago it had been populated by men who worked in the brick yards . . . good solid middle class working people. But after the war the brickyards began to close down; slowly at first, then rapidly. As the yards ran down so did the neighborhood. The people had lost the conviction of their own human dignity. There were few jobs. Little money. No hope. Seemingly no future. These people, though perhaps more sophisticated, had problems very much the same as those in the missions. The mutual concern of nun and priest resulted in Samaritan House.

Just as in the missions, human friendships would come first. People didn't learn spiritual values from words, Father Clementi had said. They wouldn't understand ethical principles because there was a cross on the hospital where they were treated. But they could learn and understand from the example of nuns living their lives by those values and principles.

They had received permission to establish Samaritan House as an experimental convent in a long abandoned school building. Sister Claire and her nuns would live there as a kind of model family, to reach people with their example, rather than preaching or teaching. They would still follow the rule of the convent that St. Dominic had founded:

"Eat as the people around you eat. Share their poverty, their suffering . . . and your love of Our Lord."

In the chapel, Sister Claire, burdened with the responsibility of Prioress for this small convent, concluded her meditation and prayed for God's blessing on Samaritan House. The small group of nuns she had were beginning to establish themselves. One more was due from the convent at Bornham. But the ting-a-ling of the bell failed to penetrate her prayers.

The largest room in Samaritan House had been set aside as a recreation room . . . in high hopes, as Sister Claire had expressed it, that they would soon have a swarm of neighbors to come and recreate. At this moment, it was a bare room, in the process of being painted. On a ladder against the wall Sister Mary's dark African face glowed in sharp contrast to her white habit. Her tongue protruded between her lips in strong concentration as she filled in the last gray area with a wide brush. Then she leaned back to admire her handiwork like Michelangelo surveying the ceiling of the Sistine chapel.

"Not bad," she mused.

Her companion, Sister Michele, less accustomed to a brush, fought a losing battle against the paint sliding down along the brush's handle. She surveyed the large patch of wall which she had managed to cover with paint with less satisfaction than Sister Mary. Some spots were lumpy with white paint, others barely covered. The marks of the brush strokes stood out clearly.

"It has a lot of texture," she shrugged.

Neither of them had noticed the first ring of the bell. But now as they regarded each other's work the second ting-a-ling startled each of them. Sister Michele automatically turned toward the door but hesitated. They looked at their smudged and perspiring selves and Sister Michele grinned.

"Think I should go? Like this?"

"We're working nuns," Sister Mary affirmed. "And that's just what we look like!"

Sister Michele moved toward the open entrance doors as the bell jangled the convent quiet for the third time.

Among the other nuns at Samaritan House, distinguished for her organizational and administrative efficiency and for the sour face she wore, was Sister Cluny. One of the younger nuns in a less charitable moment once described Sister Cluny as looking as if she had plunged both feet into a pool of cold water and bit into a sour lemon, simultaneously. It was an understatement. Long before they had come to Samaritan House Sister Cluny was well known in the Order as "Gloomy Cluny."

She had been in the kitchen. When the bell sounded for the third time, unanswered, she barrelled out into the short hall leading to the front door. Opposite the entrance was a handsome wooden stairway with a massive newel post. As she rounded this, bearing down on the front door, Sister Cluny almost collided with Sister Michele.

"I'm sorry." Sister Michele was chastened. "I should have gotten it, Sister."

Gloomy Cluny was a misnomer. She had a sour wit. "It's perfectly all right," she said drying her hands hastily on her apron. "As long as I had nothing better to do."

Sister Michele retreated into the recreation room as Sister Cluny threw open the door.

Gloomy Gluny looked out. No one was there.

She grew wary. She brought a natural suspicion to all tasks knowing that sour-faced women, especially sour-faced nuns, were destined to be teased and taunted. Children considered her their natural enemy. She stepped forward looking from side to side of the empty stoop.

"Hello . . . Hello? . . . Who rang this bell!"

Across from Samaritan House a group of young teenagers, boys and girls, stood in a line along the curb. They stared at Cluny but no one spoke. About to reenter Sister suddenly noticed the suitcase and guitar resting against the wall to one side of the door, and bent over them greatly puzzled.

"I'll be right there Sister." And almost before Sister Cluny could straighten up, Sister Ann was.

"Thought I'd better get my scooter under the shed."

Sister Cluny glanced across the street darkly and nodded "It will be much safer there." And then she was almost bowled over by the small dynamo in coif and veil who appeared from the corner of the building.

"I'm Sister Ann. Would you please hold the door for me?" She scooped up her bag and guitar. "I see it's painted already! All the way from the convent I couldn't wait to see what this place would be like." She entered through the door.

Through this whirlwind of talk and action Sister Cluny watched in confusion. Her mouth was open. She remembered to close the door as Sister Ann set her things down in the foyer and turned to greet her more formally.

"I hope I'm not late. I'm used to the scooter on country roads but these cobblestone streets!" Sister Ann jiggled herself up and down in vivid illustration. "I'm still bouncing!" She took a deep breath. "I'm glad I'm finally here Sister."

"We expected you this morning," said Sister Cluny, recovering.

"Oh, I was supposed to come by train but at the last minute Mother Superior decided you could use a scooter here, as long as I didn't mind being the delivery girl. You know the only thing that bothered me at all is that on a train all those hours you usually have someone to talk to."

Sister Cluny had an immediate vision of what a long train trip would be like alongside this volcano.

"Well, now you have *me* to talk to: Sister Cluny."

"Hello, Sister Cluny." The younger nun took her hand and greeted her warmly. "I'm glad to meet you."

This was not quite the sentiment that most people expressed about Sister Cluny. "Better late than never," she managed.

"Thank you." Sister Ann wrinkled her nose. "What's that peculiar smell?" Her face expressively recoiled against the offending aroma.

Sister Cluny sniffed the air with her ample nose. "You mean the fresh paint, Sister . . . or my stew?"

It took Sister Ann a moment to appreciate the question. Then she smiled. "Well, I *hope* I mean the fresh paint!"

Sister Claire had completed her meditation and hearing the sound of voices at the entry hall came to greet the

new arrival. She embraced the younger nun and welcomed her, taking sharp note of the lively eyes, the volu-
ble tongue, the expressive face and manner. People will
like this one, she thought to herself. This is the kind that
teenagers will confide in. This is the kind who will wade
into an overburdened family and help it pull itself up by
its own bootstraps. Yes, Sister Ann seemed to be as adver-
tised. She led her across the entry hall.

"It's the ideal spot for us, don't you think?"

Sister Ann had been drinking in her surroundings as
well as her new Prioress. "Well . . . Yes Mother. But I
didn't picture it being quite *this* 'ideal.'"

She gestured, embracing her surroundings and, raising
her arms, revealed several smudges on her habit: mud and
dirt from her tumble along the canal road earlier.

Sister Cluny was a stickler for detail and a staunch de-
fender of starched collars and snowwhite habits. She
pointed at the smudges and questioned them with the air
of St. Peter at the gates of Paradise taking note of mortal
sins.

Sister Ann glanced down at her habit. "Oh that. I have
to tell you. It was the funniest thing! I was riding along
this road, pretty fast, and a barge captain whistled at me."
Sister Cluny's frown deepened. It was worse than she
thought.

"I mean the boat whistle." That was no better.

"I mean the captain of this barge tooted the boat whistle at me." She decided to go on anyway. "But in the
other direction this bicycle was coming . . ."

Luckily the arrival of the other nuns of the community
saved her from further explanation. They came from several directions, all calling out to her at once. And Sister
Claire whispered in her ear "We'll have a good chat later.
They all want to meet you."

Sister Ann made a total of ten: Bird-like Sister Elise,
like Sister Michele and Sister Mary, just a year or two
older than Sister Ann; Sister Marie and plump Sister
Therese were contemporaries of the prioress; Sister

Cluny, of course, was ageless. Like any women meeting after a long absence, the hubbub of greetings, embraces and introductions filled the large recreation room with chatter. What was it like here? The answers were as different as the nuns who gave them. As difficulty piled on difficulty Sister Ann only smiled, then gave a long mock sigh of sympathy. "Well, Sisters," she exclaimed, "it gets tougher and tougher to save your soul every day!"

They spoke of the lonely families, of the scarcity of jobs, of the lack of contact between the people and themselves. How were they going to make contact with stonewalls? Sister Elise had hoped for meetings, classes, dances and parties, everything, all in this one big recreation room. But so far the neighbors had been about as neighborly as sharks.

Sister Ann looked around. The big bare room, with its fresh coat of paint was unfurnished except for a large old wooden table, a battered piano covered with a dropcloth and several chairs with their stuffing bulging against their upholstered covering. It did seem kind of empty.

Sister Mary quietly answered her concern. "So are the people who live here, Sister."

Sister Claire observed her young charges from the door of the recreation room, weighing each of them against the difficulties of the future. Always business, Sister Cluny had picked up the newcomer's suitcase and guitar and started for the stairs. But Sister Claire stopped her with a question.

"What do you think of her."

Gloomy Cluny made shrewd appraisals. "Talks a lot," was her instant analysis.

"She's excited. When Sister Ann volunteered I thought some of that enthusiasm of hers might be just what we need here."

Sister Cluny hefted the heavy guitar case and grunted her way up the remaining stairs. She had a final comment. "We need workers, Mother; not guitar players."

Mother Prioress explained that Sister Ann was an orphan. What Sister Cluny carried in her hands now was all the family the young nun would ever see. Sister Cluny nodded unemotionally. "Going to get noisy around here."

Mother Prioress grinned. She knew Sister Cluny too well to be taken in by a sour face. She wanted to hear more. And Sister Cluny was a woman of few words but many opinions.

"Mother, you know I have a tendency to be blunt . . ."

"I rely on that Sister Cluny."

"She seems full of enthusiasm, she plays the guitar . . . but can she *give* these people anything?"

Sister Claire watched her companion disappear at the head of the stairs. As usual Gloomy Cluny had put a finger squarely on the heart of the matter. That was the reason for their experiment, to answer that question for an entire Order of nuns.

CHAPTER III

Despite repeated rumors to the contrary, the oldest thing at Samaritan House was not Sister Cluny but a large Bible. More than 100 years ago, the Dominican sisters had carried it when they first landed in Africa. Now, the once handsome leather was corroded by mildew; its pages were smudged from perspiring fingertips, white and black, reverent and curious. Mother Superior had sent the memento to the nuns at Samaritan House to remind them that their job here was to uphold and make relevant the ancient traditions of their Order.

The evening meal was long over and the nuns had scattered about Samaritan House on their various tasks. In the kitchen, Sister Mary read from the old Bible as Sister Ann finished drying the last of an array of dishes and pots from the community's dinner.

Like everything else at Samaritan House the kitchen was adequate . . . a word by which the Sisters mean that they would survive despite any obstacles. Ancient pipes belched forth water seasoned with chemicals and rust. When she washed the dishes Sister Mary warned her companion that the water was so hard she must never allow it to fall unbroken from tap to dish for fear it would shatter even their durable cups and saucers. The oven however was huge, and suitable to cooking for ten at a time.

"Sing joyfully to God all the earth; serve ye the Lord with gladness. Come before His presence with exceeding great joy. Know ye that the Lord He is God. Enter his gates with praise, go into His courts with hymns and give glory to Him. Praise ye His name . . ." The rich voice of the dark-skinned nun filled that kitchen with a warmth no stove could give.

Enjoying the poetry of the psalms, Sister Ann turned quickly and caught one of the heavy cups with the trailing edge of her dish towel. She reached for it but her contortionist's wriggle was not enough; she only managed to deflect the heavy cup. Its crash interrupted Sister Mary.

"Well, off to an auspicious start!" Sister Ann bent to pick up the pieces.

The older, African nun was amused by her buoyant spirit. "That's nothing. My first day here I lost my balance on the ladder and spilled paint all over Gloomy Cluny!"

The young nun shuddered, picturing that austere woman through a veil of paint. "What did you do?" she wondered of her companion.

Sister Mary's eyes glowed. The first thing she had in fact done, was laugh. But now she composed her dark face to remember.

"I apologized, of course. Sister Cluny's really a good sport, so I told her it was better I did it to *her* than she did it to me . . . the paint was *whitewash!*"

As they cleaned up the pieces, Sister Ann began to speak of her love of music; always an important part of her life before and after entering the convent. The songs she liked to compose and sing she considered an act of prayer.

On her part, Sister Mary recalled her childhood in Africa. She remembered her first sight of gold and how disappointed she had been. Like most things in mission lands, she told Sister Ann, even gold didn't seem quite so bright and dazzling in its primitive state. But she loved her native land even after these long years away.

While Sister Ann dumped the pieces of the broken cup into the trash pail with a loud bang, Sister Mary fondly examined again the inscriptions in the front of the beautiful old Bible. Suddenly she wished that she could be the one to return it to Africa.

"We're guinea pigs," Sister Mary reminded her companion, "trying something new here. New methods. If they work, some of us will go to the missions and try them there too. A lot of people, Sister, the first thing they want to do is leave where they came from and go some place else. I can't wait to go back to those scrubby little villages on the plains." She paused a moment and tempered her enthusiasm. "If that's where the Order wants me to be."

Sister Ann wanted to go almost as badly. They could serve God anywhere . . . but Africa! It seemed to cry out the loudest for help.

Sister Mary understood. So much to do. So many to be helped. But she warned this newcomer that there was lots more to it. "Vultures, poisonous snakes, disease; bugs, and poverty you wouldn't believe: they're the African missions too."

Sister Ann was an optimist, and held up the last cup, as she finished drying, to illustrate it. An optimist, she explained, with half a cup of water says its still half full; the pessimist says its half empty already.

"Be an optimist here, too, Sister. We have to be the yeast in their lives. Give our love to people whose self respect has died, and they rise up full of life again."

"I'll try," promised Sister Ann.

Suddenly they were interrupted by the faint sounds of a piano and singing coming from another room. This, Sister Mary informed her friend, was the Evening Concert.

It didn't sound like a radio to Sister Ann. It wasn't. It was Gloomy Cluny.

"She only knows four songs but she plays them every night."

"And you've been here three weeks?" The thought was appalling.

"It's not so bad," Sister Mary nodded. "She plays by ear . . . so they sound a little different each time!"

The evening concert reached every recess of Samaritan House including the office of the busy Prioress. Papers, files, correspondence all covered a battered desk. A man's coat carelessly tossed over a chair partially covered a large battered tool box. It's owner was rummaging through the tools.

Full of energy and passion for his work, Father Clementi was the advisor and sparkplug of Samaritan House. Between he and the Prioress a warm affection had grown up in the weeks since Samaritan House had become not a dream but an established fact. She shook the wrinkles from his coat and hung it on a coat tree. Each thing in its proper place she thought: a respect for neatness and order which Father Clementi shared as far as his work and other people were concerned but seldom about himself. He had left his hammer on the floor when he fixed the refrigerator a few days before. Sister Claire gave him a look of mock reproof.

"You'll find it in the work room, Father."

"Strange place for a hammer, Sister. *I* would have looked on the floor next to the refrigerator."

Together they walked to the work room which Father Clementi had earlier set aside as a necessity if ever Samaritan House were to have furniture. There was considerable clutter, a good comfortable feeling of things in work. Father Clementi liked to have more than one thing going at a time. His favorite at the moment was the start of a soda fountain which he hoped would soon be the main attraction of the recreation room so the Sisters could invite teenagers for weekend dances.

Watching him set about preparations for work the Prioress recalled the first evening she had come to help him. Characteristically he had greeted her warmly, then immediately thrust the end of a plank into her hand and instructed her: "Hold this. Less talk and more work."

In the recreation room, Sister Cluny sat at the old upright, leaning back in the ham-handed playing style of those immune to the pain of dissonant chords and wobbly tempo. The room was well lighted, the home-made curtains drawn and the street windows opened for fresh air. The community of nuns enjoyed music, and the smell of fresh paint gave it a homey atmosphere to which even Father Clementi and the Prioress were soon drawn, adding a virile baritone and a quavering soprano to the sweet voices of the nuns, Sister Cluny's piano, and the guitar of Sister Ann.

They had departed from the four songs that comprised the repertoire of the usual evening concert and were following Father Clementi in a vigorous, spirited rendition of a simple little folk song called "Brother John." The song was in the form of a round; each chorus building on the last and describing Brother John with a smile, with a frown, with a tear on his face.

Sister Ann's clear, fresh voice, accompanied by her guitar, added a special zest to the singing and since several of the younger nuns and even Father Clementi had heard her sing before at Bornham they insisted that she contribute one of her own songs now.

She chose "Sister Adele." It was a little foolish she admitted for a grown woman to call a guitar by a name as if it were human. It had been a joke at first but her guitar had too many memories; it meant too much for her to stop once she had begun. The music had a flamenco beat describing how she had acquired the guitar and given it a name. Her spirit was too contagious for even Sister Cluny to resist.

Outside a few weary workmen trudged homeward in the waning light. The sound of music, the clapping hands and the joyous singing, coming like a breath of fresh air from the staid old convent building convinced them, if convincing they needed, that here, in their own neighborhood, they were witnessing some modern madness on the part of the church. What could those nuns possibly find to be so gay about?

The music continued inside, enlivening the evening. As Father Clementi listened, a seed was planted in his mind, and in that fertile ground, took root.

CHAPTER IV

No requirement for the nuns at Samaritan House had been more strictly laid down by Father Clementi and the Prioress than that they provide a suitable place and daily supervision for children to play. Cobbled streets and the debris filled yards of shuttered factories made poor playgrounds. In this neighborhood children learned to smoke, to drink and often to fight and steal at a far more tender age than they learned to read and write.

Beyond that, it was an important and simple solution to the problem of reaching the people. Nuns and a priest were unwelcome; they were often thought to be so deeply concerned with the spiritual world that they were strangers to the demanding reality of this one. Before the nuns could be a model family, before they could share anything with these people, before they could hope to show them the meaning of a true Christian love, they had to have contact with them. Short of tripping them up in the street or knocking on doors, it seemed unlikely at first that this contact ever could be made.

But a playground was a practical and much appreciated offering to the neighborhood. As they got to know the children, they soon would get to know the families of those children. Once contact was made it was up to them to win friendship.

To the rear of Samaritan House was the paved yard of the old school. Cleared of debris and rubble the Sisters had started a small garden, for their kitchen and for the delight of seeing things grow. Father Clementi had made a few tables, and as an accomplishment he considered second only to his ordination, he had persuaded some manufacturers to donate play equipment. What thrilled the children at first was the garden.

Watching nuns hoeing the hard earth and planting things, the children had jeered. Their experience with nature was that things died, things grew worn with use and crusted with age. To them it was an unrivaled surprise when small green shoots first poked their way up out of the ground and greeted them as living examples of hope and faith. The older ones were still stand-offish, fearful of the derision of their friends and clinging to the small security of a group. But the small ones came.

On this bright morning Sister Mary sat at one of the tables explaining the game of jacks to a group of puzzled but curious little girls. The colored nun offered not only her warm personality but the novelty of her dark skin. They were shy at first. Then soon they were grabbing for the jacks and the little rubber ball with total disregard for the strange white robes, the unusual dark skin or even their natural distrust of adults.

On the blacktopped pavement a group of 6 to 8 year old boys played soccer with Sister Ann. It was a no-holds-barred, victory-or-death contest the way they played it. The children utterly disregarded the fact that she was an adult, a female and a nun. Sister Ann ignored those handicaps, too.

An urchin in short pants, Dominic Arlien, nursed the ball toward the goal defended by Sister Ann's team. He was smaller than some of the others but he made up for his size in determination and toughness.

"Hey, Dom, here! Here!"

He attempted to pass the ball to the boy who called for it but Sister Ann intercepted and started across the field. Dom was frantic. "Get it," he yelled. "Get it."

The ball became the focus of all his energy, all his attention. Now Sister Ann, gaining control of the soccer ball, maneuvered it straight toward Dom and his teammates who stood between her and the goal. She dribbled it adeptly preparing for a kick aimed at the goal. But just as she was about to make her shot, Dom came running in close, swung his foot back and booted her, straight and square, just below the shin.

"Oww!" she danced on one foot, grasping the leg in both hands. "My leg!"

She was the only witness to this agony. All the boys, her own team and opponents, concentrated all their attention on the ball. One injured player, more or less, nun or not, counted for nothing compared to a score.

The ball, wobbling erratically along the ground as she lost control of it, was easily captured by Dom's team and, led by the small boy with adept footwork, they managed to bring it into position. Dom's aim this time was just as true as it was on Sister Ann. He kicked a goal.

In the center of the field Sister Ann half hopped, half held her leg. Still heedless, the two teams began to re-form. Spotting the little boy who had just managed two successful kicks in a row, the nun called. "You, Arlien, come here a minute."

The boy trotted up and limping painfully she managed to catch one small hand. "I want to talk to you young man."

Dom was one of those boys with eyes so large and bright they stood out from his face like two glowing candles in a darkened room. Despite the toughness he assumed, he could have posed for the seraphim or cherubim in a Renaissance painting. He looked up at her in total innocence. "Hurt your leg, huh?"

"Yes, I wonder how!" Together they had reached a bench near the entry gate which held the children's sweaters, odds and ends, and her own guitar. She cleared a space and sat down. The boy watched her, wary now.

"Maybe you tripped over your skirt."

Sister Ann bent over her leg and raised the skirt to examine the tender spot with her fingers.

"My skirt doesn't leave black and blue marks."

The boy stared at her shoes and the long white stockings. Curiosity overcame caution.

"You got awful long skirts!"

"What I need, is a suit of armor."

Dominic edged away, propelled not only by guilt but by the strangeness of this woman and her peculiar clothes.

"Well," he fumbled, "I gotta get back to the game."

The others had drifted toward them in a small circle, impatiently waiting for the game to resume and wondering what she would do. Sister Ann beckoned Dominic close with one finger, leaned down to his ear and whispered: "Dominic Arlien, did you kick me?"

Dom squirmed under her direct gaze. Unwilling to lie he glanced to one side then the other, then back to his cronies, seeking a getaway. There was none.

"They're waiting, Sister . . ."

Sister Ann kept a gentle grip on his arm. "You haven't answered me, Dominic." There was no answer. "Do you know you are named after a great man?"

"Who?" Dom was suspicious of the change of subject.

Quietly and simply she told him there was a rugged fellow just like him. A fighter; a fighter for good things because they were right, and not only because he wanted to win: St. Dominic. He had worn clothes the same as Sister Ann's and Father Clementi. Dominic frowned.

"How did he play soccer?"

Sister Ann didn't laugh. It was a perfectly natural question. "Same as me, Dom. Only better, of course."

The teams grew impatient. Were they going to play or not? Sister Ann begged time for a small rest and as the boys began to scuttle on, she reached for her guitar and removed it from the case. Dom edged away, not sure if he was released. But as he was about to turn and head for the field Sister Mary summoned all of them. Mothers had come. It was time to go home. The game reluctantly abandoned, the boys raced pell mell toward the gate where their mothers waited to welcome them and take them home. The nuns made no effort to force themselves on the mothers but greeted those who greeted them. Out of the corner of her eye Sister Ann noted the last of the boys racing off still clutching the soccer ball.

"The ball," she called after him. "Leave the ball." Caught in the act, the lad tossed the ball back toward her without losing stride and galloped off to his waiting mother.

Dom stood at a little distance, waiting still, the only boy whose mother had not come, though several girls still remained with Sister Mary. Making no effort to call him, Sister Ann instead began to play and sing one of her songs, a song which told the story of their founder St. Dominic.

The boy at first feigned indifference, then came closer on the pretext of looking at someone coming through the gate, until for the final chorus he stood listening almost directly in front of her.

She looked him over. Dom looked down at the ground. And then Sister Ann began her song again, bending toward him and ad libbing, talking the words as she played the accompanying chords.

The words trailed off into silence and the boy looked at her. He smiled. But before he could speak he was summoned from the gate.

Nicole Arlien was 17. She wore no makeup, a simple skirt and sweater, but she looked older.

"I gotta go," Dominic gestured, "It's my sister."

He started off and Sister Ann watched him. The girl

seemed like most of the others in this neighborhood and yet . . . before he had gone more than a few paces the little boy suddenly stopped, slowly turned around and came back to her. The two large dark eyes looked forthrightly into hers. He swallowed.

"I kicked ya on purpose." It was a whisper of confession.

Sister Ann whispered her reply, "I know."

As Dominic turned and hustled off he almost bumped into his sister. Was there something wrong, the girl wanted to know. But Sister Ann reassured her. No. Dominic had just been saying goodbye. Nicole looked from the boy to the nun aware that something had passed between these two. Sister Ann took advantage of the opportunity to introduce herself, and searching for a neutral question asked where she worked.

"I'm a maid, Sister." Nicole shrugged. "Not many places around here to work. Especially for a maid. Thanks again." She nudged her brother. "Say goodbye to Sister."

"Bye."

The two of them started off, but Dominic turned back over his shoulder. "See you tomorrow, Sister."

It was meant as a peace offering. Sister acknowledged it.

"See you tomorrow, Dominic."

She watched them disappear. It was a strange exchange. So little had been said and yet she was aware a great deal had been said without words. Sister Ann was a forthright person. She was unsure, perhaps even unperceptive in this kind of conversation. Her self appraisal was cut short by the appearance of Father Clementi.

"Where were you, Father? I could have used a good goalie."

Father Clementi indicated the convent. "Giving Mother Prioress a sales pitch."

Father had news. At their songfest a few evenings before he had told Sister Ann that he wanted some records of her songs. Not only for himself, but to send to other convents of nuns. They were the sort of thing he felt that other Dominicans would enjoy. Now he had found where to get them: Primavera Records.

"Primavera?" Sister Ann was surprised. It was a very prominent company.

Father Clementi was a born salesman. He had persuaded a friend at the recording company in Ghent to let them use one of the small recording booths. It wouldn't take long. "Then we can send records to all the convents of the Dominican Order."

"Father," Sister Ann laughed, "Why do you do everything in such half-way measures?"

It didn't take much persuasion, now, though Sister Ann had never recorded anything even at the Conservatory; it sounded like too much fun to resist. Especially since Father Clementi promised to come down and give her moral support along with some of the other sisters. He had already hurtled the greatest obstacle: Mother Prioress had given her consent.

Perhaps she would not have consented so readily had she pictured her young nuns following Father Clementi toward the large Primavera building at a busy street in Ghent: he looked like a white robed pied-piper, leading three white mice instead of children. They stared up at the huge sign atop the multi story building in the heart of the city, then moved to the corner opposite the entrance.

The traffic was heavy. Sisters Michele, Ann, and Mary stepped off the curb but the cars whizzed by, tooting horns to force them back on the sidewalk. Finally a policeman crossed from his perch in the center of the street and seeing their trouble blew his whistle raising his hand palm out. When the cars screeched to a halt he gestured for the group to cross. Passing him in the center of the street Sister Ann carrying her guitar with some difficulty, made a small bow of acknowledgment. The policeman smiled and returned the bow, adding a salute.

He was not a Catholic, but as long as he was king of

this street, as long as the responsibility and the authority rested in his white gloved hands he would show these drivers who was boss. He waited till all four were completely across the street and on the other sidewalk. Then he blew his whistle, waved both arms for the flow of traffic to begin again. But he had made a mistake. In calling to the nuns and the priest he had stepped down from his island of safety, his white painted throne of authority, and found himself now in the center of the street. The cars trapped him.

He blew his whistle, shrilly; he shook his fist at them; he shouted. But in the swirling sea of traffic and the roar of horns he was but a grain of sand. He cursed under his breath and then at the top of his voice, though no one could hear him. That's what happened to a man when he tried to do a good deed!

Unaware that their benefactor had been caught in the center of the maelstrom behind them, the Sisters and Father Clementi moved toward the entrance doors and were swallowed up by the huge maw of Primavera Records.

The receptionist's desk in the vast ante-room was unattended. It was a room furnished with taste; more like a salon than an office waiting room, except for the display of album covers along one wall. Various hopefuls overflowed the furniture around the room. The babble of their conversation stopped at the sight of the nuns but resumed almost instantly. Long white robes, the coifs and veils, seemed less strange to them than these strange people seemed to the nuns.

A business man shuffled a deck of papers into his attache case; a jazz combo stood in one corner letting their beards grow; a boy-girl team, dressed identically in cowboy jeans, shorts and hats tried to seem blasé; a homely pianist in a dinner jacket nervously massaged his long thin fingers. For all of them the future lay between the grooves of a round, black plastic disc.

While the Sisters edged their way through this throng with many "excuse me's" to a corner of the room where they would feel less conspicuous, Father Clementi strode over to the receptionist's desk.

The desk guarded two rich wooden doors with an elegant sign: Executive Offices. Behind the desk the very chic receptinist poised her fingers over a row of buttons on a very modern inter-com. Father Clementi insisted that he was expected.

"Would you call Mr. Girarde *out* of conference please?"

She protested. It was the weekly staff meeting and it had been impressed upon her when she was hired that the last time a receptionist had summoned an executive from the weekly staff conference it had been to inform him of the invasion of the lowlands by Hitler's army. Father Clementi had been turned down by experts. He had bounced back in the face of thunderous no's; he had turned the cheek to insults till he felt like a whirling dervish; he had cut through enough red tape to wrap all of Belgium as a Christmas gift: he was not to be put off now. With his most persuasive grin he reminded her of their appointment and of how far they had come to keep it.

"Just tell him there's a character in a Roman collar out here making a big fuss . . . and I'll apologize for both of us."

The nuns sat patiently on a couch. Crossing the room directly toward them came a quartet of haughty young men in costume for a corrida complete to the coil of hair at the nape of the neck, swords and capes. Three of them flopped into chairs across from the nuns.

The last of the group stopped just before Sister Ann, paused to take in the room and especially the Sisters. He was an arrogant young man, the kind who believed all women's hearts palpitated at his every breath. He eyed Sister Ann. His gaze took in the guitar propped up on the end of the couch beside her, swung back to the woman. Then he gave her his special smile; almost a wink.

Sister Ann had been brought up with a stern appreciation of being polite. Lately at Samaritan House she was accustomed to making a particular effort at friendliness. She smiled back.

The matador's confidence grew. "Hello, there."

"Hello." she returned.

He took a step closer, reached the pack of cigarettes inside his waistband. "Smoke?"

"No thank you."

He was used to some little delay in making his conquests. Women liked to make a pretense of not surrendering too soon. He smiled. "What's the name of your act?"

"The act?" It took her a moment to understand. Caught off guard she answered the question with a question. "What's yours?"

He tossed it off with a flirtatious smile. "The Mad Matadors."

Sister Ann was not to be outdone. "We're the Dominican Delinquents." Before he could reply Sister Mary beckoned her companions. Sister Ann nodded and bent to pick up her guitar. But the matador handed it to her with a conquering grin.

"Thank you."

He turned the charm on to full throttle. "See you later . . ."

He watched the three women cross toward the reception desk and his eye settled on Father Clementi. His jaw fell. He stared after the four figures in white disappearing through the doors, then jerked his head back to the bench with growing awareness and embarrassment. He looked at the nuns and priest again, then down at his own costume and stared after them with a sickly smile of disbelief. His moment of truth had come.

As Robert Gerarde led the Sisters and Father Clementi down a corridor past a glass-enclosed master control room his thoughts were on the meeting from which he had just been summoned. Covering his annoyance with his standard quip to new visitors to Primavera he indicated the audition studios. "Dante wrote 'Abandon hope all ye who enter here' . . . but hope usually begins in these rooms."

In his rush he had barely acknowledged the introductions to the three nuns. Now he was brought up short as one of them filing past him while he held open the door to a studio marked "D" spoke in a vaguely familiar voice.

"Imagine Mr. Gerarde if we'd had such facilities at the Conservatory."

Five years ago when the girl who became Sister Ann had entered the Brussels Conservatory of Music the student god, boy genius, and resident rake had been the 22 year old son of a distinguished French family, Robert Gerarde. He wrote music sporadically; but to escapades, parties and flamboyant school stunts he had devoted himself with diligence. A few years ago, his training long since completed, yet still without a finished work by which to gauge his talent, Robert's father had offered to subsidize the time for an original work with one string attached: the young man would first prove his maturity in steady employment for at least 12 months.

A stimulating job had been found working with new and experimental musical artists for the largest recording firm in Belgium, Primavera Records. To the delight of all concerned Robert became a success; to his own satisfaction, the work developed in him a sense of discipline. Part of the reason for Robert's success lay in his ability to recognize artistic talent and provide constructive criticism. But many men had that. Robert's strength was a sophisticated, dashing charm, handsome appearance, a fashionable existentialism that supported his instinct to discover all the zest in living and pluck it for himself and those around him to savour. Robert Gerarde was in fact a man most people found irresistible.

Frustrated by the inability to achieve anything in his own work and his own life, he lately had shucked off the boyish egotism that made him foolish in school but retained all the qualities which made him a most appealing natural leader. The relationship about to develop between such a man of the world and Sister Ann would provide an even greater challenge.

How could he have failed to recognize her?

"I'm five years older Robert."

Politely, but with cynical amusement he apologized. "To tell you the truth . . . in all those robes . . . I have trouble telling one nun from another!"

"It's easy," Sister Ann introduced her companions. "This is Sister Michele; Sister Mary; I'm Sister Ann."

"You haven't changed," he laughed. "What fun we had . . . if you'll forgive my familiarity, sisters."

"I'm a nun, not an amnesia victim!"

They both laughed; and the laughter began to bridge five years.

Did she still recall the time he took her to that wild beatnik joint? Or hocking her guitar to pay Robert's bail after one of his notorious three day weekends? Despite a generous allowance from his family he was permanently broke. She remembered. All of it.

But the staff meeting could be postponed only so long. Much as he would have liked to continue their conversation Robert had to leave. Imagine after all those years finding Lucienne, the ebullient, beautiful and romantic girl he once dated, buried in some musty solemn convent. Nevertheless he was delighted to see her again anyway. He told her of his work here at Primavera.

"I discover new artists, groom their careers, making certain their affection for Primavera Records is undying . . . and legally binding! But you a nun!" He couldn't get over it.

"What do you intend to record?"

Sister Ann's answer confirmed his opinion of nuns. They had several songs, her own compositions. One about the founder of their Order, St. Dominic. And one about her happiness in her vocation.

"Her songs are so interesting." Sister Mary was loyalty itself.

"Prayers, in fact." Sister Michele was not to be outdone.

Robert smiled weakly, his worst fears confirmed; he began a hasty retreat. They'd have to excuse him. So busy today. He'd love to hear them, but the staff conference could not be kept waiting. The engineer would take good care of them.

"It's good to see you again . . . Sister." No matter how long he looked at her he still saw Lucienne. "And good luck with your . . . hymns!"

The recording session resembled pious hymn singing about as much as Sister Ann's motor scooter resembled a heavenly chariot. They sang "Dominique." Sister Ann stood with one foot on a chair to help support her guitar; the other two beside her joining on the chorus. Twenty minutes after they had begun the engineer was humming along with them, touching first fingertip to thumb making a round "O" sign of approval. The rhythm was lilting, the lyrics light, the melody catchy. Sister Ann sang unaffectedly, leading them with the vigor of a hootenanny.

No one was more completely caught up in the spirit of the singing than Father Clementi. When Sister Ann was satisfied with her performance, and the engineer with all the technical details, the session seemed to be over. The engineer closed the Sisters' mike and turned to his equipment. But Father Clementi was not a man of small dreams and short vision.

"They might as well record something else, don't you think?" he hinted. "Records have two sides . . ."

The executive staff meeting was again in session. Robert sat staring at the pad in front of him doodling, while Mr. Duvries, the company president, expanded on their plans for the next five years.

Robert's mind was five years away, but it was going in the opposite direction. He resolved to listen to those records, hymns or not.

On his pad he sketched a face, and around it, the simple white hood of a nun.

CHAPTER V

"You got a handkerchief, Sister?"

"Need one, Dominic?"

Dominic shook his head. "Uh-uh."

They walked along a rough grimy section near Samaritan House where soot from the kilns had given everything a patina of gray and rust. Dominic's left eye was rimmed by a spectacular shiner of which he was very proud. He skipped along, sometimes in front of her, sometimes matching stride for stride with her as now. What puzzled him was her habit.

"Well, I have a handkerchief if you do need one . . ."

Finally Dominic blurted out his question. Where did she keep it, since she had no pockets. Sister Ann protested. She did too have pockets and she showed him the slit in her outer cloak, through which her hand could reach that pocket.

"Hey, you could hide a lot of stuff in there!"

"I do!"

She extracted a rosary and a pick for her guitar. The string of beads with its small silver cross was hand carved and since she had been a nun but a short time, the caress of finger tips counting beads had not yet worn away their lustre. Dominic held it out at arm's length examining first the beads, then the entire string. His experience with such things was limited.

"A necklace is for girls!" He returned it disdainfully.

"It isn't a necklace. It's to help say my prayers."

The little boy fingered the beads again. "You could count on your fingers." The bond of friendship had grown between them so quickly that he could add a confession. "That's what I do."

Sister Ann smiled. "Sometimes I say so many prayers Dominic, that I run out of fingers!"

Dominic was awed. He took in the thought of so much praying. But what impressed him even more was the admission by this adult that she could "run out of fingers." With honest camaraderie and no thought of insult he looked up into the nun's face.

"You're not very smart, huh, Sister?"

"Not very," she admitted.

They arrived at the Arlien home, a run down one-story building crowded on each side by abandoned warehouses. Dominic's thoughts returned to what had brought them here in the first place. He poked one small finger gently over the swollen cheek bone and hoped that it was still nice and purple.

"I'd say more . . . bluish," the nun examined his face with concern. "Does it hurt very much?"

The boy assumed his best martyred air and insisted that the pain was very minor: he indicated a vague area from hairline to chin. At this moment the door swung open and Nicole stepped out.

She was a different girl from when Sister Ann had last seen her. She wore her best dress . . . a half size too tight; her hair was arranged to make her appear older; most strikingly she wore exaggerated make-up. She jumped, seeing them . . . but was immediately drawn to the boy's eye.

Under her motherly attention, Dom squirmed, brush-

46

ing off Sister Ann's apology for the misdirected soccer
ball and brusquely insisting he be left alone. Sister Mary
had looked at him before they left and with a nurse's caution advised that it might be wise to take him home and
let him rest. Nicole agreed. Then she checked her watch,
and hesitated, suddenly aware of her appearance. She
could not stay yet she did not want the nun to stay either.

With an awkward excuse and the assurance that their
father would be home soon the girl darted off down the
street, as if removing herself from the scene would blot
out the way she looked. Employment for a maid in that
area might be difficult; but no maid went to work looking
like that. Nagged by suspicions about the girl, Sister Ann
entered the Arlien home.

It was no better inside than outside. A cramped entry;
to one side a grimy kitchen in which remnants of breakfast were still visible; and opposite, a living room with a
studio bed for Mr. Arlien. Down a short hall Dominic
led her to a bedroom. Nothing about the place seemed
unusual to him; it was simply the place where he lived.

Looking at the room made Sister Ann sad. This room
mirrored the hopelessness of those who lived in it. There
was an old brass bed, pitted with rust and the bed clothes
unmade; Dominic's small cot, also unmade. Various children's things lay about haphazardly. Nicole had left her
underthings and a dress there when she changed to go
out. A battered chest with drawers half open and a
chipped mirror was where she kept her array of cheap
cosmetics. What saddened Sister Ann was this blueprint
of lives being led without purpose.

Dominic threw himself on his cot, wrinkling his nose
at the smell of Nicole's cheap perfume.

"Phew! That stuff she uses . . . You're a lady, but you
don't stink like one, Sister!"

Sister Ann gravely thanked him for the compliment
and then suggested that the two of them surprise his sister. Dominic was suspicious of surprises and his suspicions
were confirmed when Sister Ann explained that together

they could straighten things up. When Nicole came home from work it would be all done.

"What do you say, Dominic?"

The boy surveyed the room, carefully appraising the amount of work. He considered the pros and cons and then pleasantly responded.

"I say . . . no."

She urged him on, suppressing a laugh at his honesty. She persuaded, she insisted, she cajoled. And just as he was running out of excuses he remembered his best one.

"My eye. It's starting to hurt," he covered his face with his hands. "Ooooo!"

Sister Ann recognized a superior opponent when she saw one. "What if I do the work and you keep me company?"

The boy peered through the fingers covering his face. "That wouldn't hurt too much, Sister. Just watching."

She tousled his hair. "That's what I thought."

She set to work, making beds, picking up clothing and at the same time chatting with Dominic. The boy's father would be home soon; not home from work, he hadn't worked since the brickyard closed. Home from his rounds of aimless wandering and drinking which the boy described in an obvious quote from his father as "His daily quota of 'no.'"

Dominic lay back on his bed, propped himself up on one elbow and played with Sister's guitar pick. First he held it over his bruised eye like a pirate's eye patch; taking a rubber band from his pocket he stretched it over thumb and pinky and plucked it with the pick.

She described "Sister Adele" for him: the worn spot on the handle where she held it so firmly, the dark stain near the opening of the hollow end where her father's cigarette ash once had fallen and burned a memory. He was dead many years now but her guitar recalled him more vividly and more happily than any photograph.

She picked up Nicole's shoes and moved to the crowded closet to place them on the shelf. Sister Ann was a happy worker. She described for Dominic the small but profound satisfaction to be found even in a task like straightening the room. It was a pleasure she had discovered as a small child, when her father had taught her to hoe the weeds from their garden. She rebelled against the chore, as he rebelled today, but as she chopped, disposing of each intruding weed and leaving the vegetables free to grow, she began to sense the fitness in leaving fresh turned earth and ordered rows of plants where before the choked chaos of neglected weeds had reigned. Didn't the room begin to seem more comfortable? Beds made, floor unlittered, odds and ends put away, or neatly stacked: Dominic looked about him, appreciating her appeal for neatness and order despite a small boy's innate need for clutter.

Swinging away from the shoes on the closet shelf her elbow caught the edge of a large manilla mailing envelope, knocking it to the floor. She bent to retrieve it. In the upper left hand corner was:

MODERN MODELS
6 ART POSES 6

It was followed by a local address. The flap was unsealed. Dislodged by the fall, several of the 8 x 10 glossies inside protruded about half their length from the open envelope.

Sister Ann took the envelope in both hands and came face to face with the top photograph. The girl, back to camera in the photograph, was naked, peaking seductively over her shoulder. The face, eyebrows pencilled, hair falling with artfully designed carelessness over one eye, cheeks heavily rouged, lips pouting, was unmistakably the face of Nicole Arlien.

Sister Ann was dimly aware of Dominic prattling some little boy tale as she stepped into the concealment of the closet, deliberated for a moment, then withdrew all of the photos.

Neither of them was aware of the gaunt man opening

his front door, stepping into the kitchen and settling himself heavily in a chair.

Mr. Alien was fuzzy but not drunk. In his right hand he carried a paper sack with a bottle of cheap gin, but in his heart he carried the agony of a man who drinks to forget. He lifted the bottle from its sack. He wanted it, needed it. But his eye was caught by the squalor of the room. The kitchen was small, dingy and depressing. It was not only the coat of grime and the flaking plaster of a room left unpainted for five years, but the complete absence of small touches that make of a room with doors and windows a real place to live. No curtain softened the glass window. No cloth or flowers brightened the table. In the cracked glass of the cabinet above the sink he saw his reflection. Suddenly he remembered a man long forgotten: Paul Jamie.

In the war Mr. Arlien had recovered consciousness in a hospital, relieved to find that he had suffered a minor shrapnel wound. But in the bed next to him he saw Paul Jamie. And he would never forget that name. He knew nothing else about him, except what he could see. Paul Jamie was conscious but he never spoke; he stared unendingly at the ceiling. Both arms and both legs were amputated.

Mr. Arlien saw Paul Jamie staring back at him from the glass of the closet door. He still had arms and legs but he knew he was less than a whole man.

The image blurred in the glass and Mr. Arlien raised himself with effort from the chair. He took the bottle and brought it to the sink. Then with a great effort of will, he slowly tipped the bottle until it poured. It was hard to do, but he kept pouring until it was empty. The act drained him, as well as the bottle. With shaking hand he lifted the bottle to look his tormentor in the face at his moment of victory. But it slipped from his fingers and smashed to the floor.

In the bedroom the sound alerted both Sister Ann and Dominic. The boy jumped from the bed.

"Papa's home!"

He rushed out. Sister Ann hurriedly stuffed the photos back into the envelope and followed him. The boy ran into the kitchen and thrust his small face in front of his father's, gesticulating toward his swollen eye.

"Hi, papa. See what I got?"

The man's eyes were closed, but they flew open in shocked surprise when he heard the woman's voice behind him.

"Mr. Arlien, I'm Sister Ann. I'd like to talk to you, please."

He tried to gather himself together, fighting off successive waves of alcohol, self pity and anger at this invasion of his privacy.

"Where did you come from?"

"Samaritan House. On the Rue St. Helene."

"She brought me home because I got this black eye. See? It's getting purple like your finger that time you caught it in the car door. Remember, papa? The ball hit me right there when she kicked it, but I didn't cry or anything. And she's got a guitar, too. You should hear it!"

It was too much all in one long string. The man conquered his dizziness by sitting down and waving the boy off.

"Wait a minute. Wait. I walk in, everybody's talking at once." He took the boy's hand. "Take it easy, son."

For the first time he focused clearly on the nun and frowned, noting that it was not even one of those motherly plump ones with ample shoulders to cry on. No. It was a fresh-faced, eager girl.

"What do you want here, Sister?"

She saw the fragments of the bottle on the floor and she could smell the gin. Still shaken by her first sight of the photographs she answered in a voice loud enough to still the thunderous pumping of her own heart.

"Dominic, go outside a moment please. I want to talk to your father alone. Be a good boy, just for a few minutes."

The boy looked from one to the other puzzled. His father's moods he knew were variable. But this abrupt change in the nun seemed harsh. She was pointing to the door.

"Do what I tell you, Dominic."

Dominic shrugged and went out. Arlien rose from the table and straightening up, felt his authority.

"Hey, whose house do you think this is!"

Sister Ann thrust the manilla envelope into his hand, "I found these when I started to straighten up your daughter's room."

"Who told you to come nosing around here?"

"Look, Mr. Arlien, look at these!"

He was startled and angered by her peremptory manner. "Who do you think you are? You come in here, tell my boy what to do like he was a piece of the furniture and now you try the same on me?" He grabbed the envelope and tossed it on the table behind him without looking. "Get out of here, Sister-what-ever-your-name-is!"

She stood her ground and the small explosion that had been building within her from her first sight of the photograph could be contained no longer. "I'm not leaving! You ought to be disgusted with yourself. Ashamed! I don't know . . . even what to say to you! Look what's in that envelope. I've never seen anything like . . . it's your own daughter!" She felt herself losing control, pushed past him reaching toward the envelope on the table. "Are you blind? Drunk? Open your eyes and take a good look!"

Her movement was a challenge and he took her arm whirling her back toward him. It was too much. Another day of failure, another day of cheerless drinking, another day coming home to this miserable building that never deserved the name home, but rather prison. Another day facing those two children, his only holds on sanity. Another day seeing his failures reflected in their eyes and in their emaciated bodies, but never in their words to him. Then the frightening memory of that maimed man and the insight to his own state of growing self destruction, whittling away at his strength and dignity. He had struck back. He had summoned his courage and thrown up a defense, pouring the numbing gin down the sink. And now this nun invaded his home attacking him, assailing his senses with her meaningless insults. He was still a man. He was still the master of his own home.

"Nobody walks in my house and tells me what to do: nobody. Especially not some sweet-and-holy-kid-nun that can't tell my kitchen from her own damn convent!"

He was propelling her toward the door. "You can't. You have to see those . . ."

"Get out Sister." He opened the door, "Don't come back!"

"But the photos. Nicole . . ."

"Out!" He ejected her and slammed the door.

She stood outside a moment, dazed and very embarrassed; close to tears. Dominic was not there, but a few doors down curious neighbors stared. She closed her eyes and gained control, then with lowered head, walked swiftly down the street toward Samaritan House.

In the kitchen, Arlien plopped himself down in the chair, his anger spent, his strength ebbing.

"Fool nun. Who does she think she is?"

He saw the envelope and reached for it. It lay face down on the table and he pulled it in front of him opening the flap as he did so. He reached one hand inside and slid out one of the photos. The white backing of the cheap photograph was stamped with a number and a date. He turned it over, shiny side up and stared. He held it in both hands. The photograph snapped into sharp focus in front of him.

A cry clutched at his body and died on his lips.

"Oh my God!"

CHAPTER VI

"Gerarde, I don't care if we distribute the Angel Gabriel blowing trumpet in a jazz combo, as long as it sells."

Mr. Duvries handed the freshly cut disc back to Robert. It was a dub transcribed directly from a tape, rather than pressed from a master. Covering the center was a plain paper label marked in pen SISTER ANN. Robert took the record.

"I've played this six times in the past couple of days. It haunts me. It runs through my head when I'm trying to go to sleep."

"Fine. We'll sell to insomniacs. Robert, who do you think will buy some crank nun singing holy songs?"

"Men, women, children; everyone who hears it."

Duvries was a busy man. He had no time to listen to even the careful selection of new recording artists that Robert from time to time presented to him. In truth he cared little for any music: in his own home he much preferred good conversation and good wine. And any music less than one hundred years old or performed by fewer than 50 musicians he lumped into a single category: "Fad." But Duvries was a good businessman and he had considerable faith in Robert Gerarde.

"Nuns . . . they're supposed to stay poor, aren't they, Robert?"

Robert grinned at the sly question. "Poor, not ignorant, sir. We'll still have to pay royalties to the Order."

"But she's an unknown."

"I'll negotiate a low percentage."

"Gerarde, would you be interested in working for a commission on sales of the records you recommend rather than salary?"

"If you let me begin with this."

"All right, begin," Duvries committed himself. "But Robert . . . you may also *end* with your singing nun."

Sister Ann herself felt the difficulty of beginning. Old enough to recognize the demands of self-discipline yet young enough and woman enough to feel the tears in her eyes, she sat facing Sister Claire in the Prioress's office. Failure itself was not so heavy a burden; she had failed before in tasks she had set herself to do. The difficulty lay in recognizing that her failure with the Arliens came not from their unwillingness to accept her, nor from events over which she had no control, but directly from herself. She had explained it all to her superior, sparing no detail, blaming herself, seeking spiritual advice as well as emotional absolution.

Sister Claire collected her thoughts. She felt a particular kinship with this young nun and as she looked at the eager face across the desk, the troubled eyes, yet the determined set of her mouth, she recognized in that face a mirror of herself. Different backgrounds, yes; yet many of the same traits: stubborn, full of zeal, loving God. The trouble with being a Prioress was that young nuns came to you as people go to a vending machine. They punched the proper button and expected you would deliver: sympathy, criticism, advice. Yet how was she to take the experience and learning of hard years as a nun and as a human being and turn them into words which might explain what had just happened to Sister Ann. You couldn't say as her doctor-father might have, when awakened in the middle of the night, "Take two aspirin and come around in the morning." No such thing as spiritual aspirin. Sister Ann still waited.

A nun's vows denied her a family of her own, in order that she might have room and a mother's personal love of those for whom she labored. All these people, Sister Claire told her, must be your family. If she thought of them that way, it would be easier to understand them; easier to speak to them, easier to love them for what they were, instead of scolding them for what they ought to be. The Prioress smiled. It seemed an overwhelming defeat now but all Sister Ann had to do was learn to talk to this new family of hers without putting her foot in her mouth.

Sister Ann's natural spirits returned; self-pity was as inappropriate to her as a bikini. Her superior recalled the name of their convent and the gospel story that inspired it.

A certain man fell among thieves, and lying there beaten and robbed, he was ignored or shunned by the passers-by until an outcast in that neighborhood, a social pariah, saw his neighbor and came to his rescue. He bound up his wounds, lifted him to his donkey and brought him to an inn where he paid his bills in advance. This man was a Samaritan and the point of the story had been that though he was a stranger he had recognized as his neighbor any man who needed help. Nicole was Sister Ann's neighbor; so was Mr. Arlien.

Listening to her own words, Sister Claire had a flash of insight; simple truths are never platitudes; they only become commonplace because we fail to live them profoundly.

Outside Samaritan House two travelers approached in a Mercedes so shiny that it made the neighborhood seem even more drab and tarnished. Between Robert and Father Clementi on the front seat was one of Sister Ann's recordings, plus a thick typewritten contract.

"The point is, Father, why should they be limited to convents and nuns?"

"Keep talking, Robert. You're convincing me."

"Think what the money could mean to this Samaritan House of yours."

"I could buy nails." The priest noticed Robert's puzzled frown. "I had to stop building a soda fountain because I ran out of nails.

"You'll buy a lot more than nails, Father! It's a calculated risk, of course. Unless the record sells big the royalties would amount to nothing."

"Nothing?" Father Clementi switched from reluctant buyer to enthusiastic seller. "Everyone will buy those records. They're great! We might make enough to finance our experiment in Africa, too. Besides, Robert, her songs have a good end in themselves, even if there were no money involved."

"Keep talking, Father," Robert grinned as he pulled up at Samaritan House. "You're convincing me."

The recreation room was still very bare, but aside from a new coat of paint and chairs and the piano it now boasted a torn billiard table. Father Clementi might run out of money, but on his frequent forays to would-be-benefactors he made a point of insisting that he could make use of almost anything at Samaritan House. It was a good approach, for Father Clementi was a difficult man to say no to. To say that you had absolutely nothing you could spare required either glacial indifference or an ability to lie, so confirmed, that not even Father Clementi's piercing eyes would ever make you smell brimstone or feel fire.

This billiard table was one man's attempt to test Father Clementi's plea that they would take "anything." To his enormous surprise, the priest had smiled his thanks and arranged to have the billiard table delivered. At first the nuns had laughed and Mother Prioress had frowned severely, until Father himself arrived to explain that it was just the thing to attract teenagers to their first dance. Gloomy Cluny wryly observed that they might as well go all the way and stage a burlesque show with free drinks on the side if they really wanted to draw a crowd. But now that the evening for the dance was approaching and word had gone out in the neighborhood, even she agreed that a billiard table seemed a good idea.

In the center of the room reaching up to the high ceiling from a step ladder, Sister Ann put the last of three paper streamers in place. The effect drew more attention to the naked corner than to the three which were decorated. She would have to find something. Down the ladder she came, then started across the floor. But as she moved past the billiard table she was attracted to it. Several balls rested on the soiled felt where the deliveryman had left them. There was a cue as well. She picked it up, puzzled by the heavy weighted end and the smooth chalked tip. It felt natural in her hand. Sister Ann looked over each shoulder to see she was alone. She couldn't resist.

Her eyes sighted along the loosely held cue lining up the shot. She squinted one eye, calculating the trajectory of one ball and its impact on the next with the blind confidence of an amateur. With an imaginary line drawn straight from her cue tip to the first ball she was ready. Yet, try as she would she could not find the proper way to grasp the cue so that she controlled its movement.

She rolled it over several times, trying first to mount the cue on the carriage of her knuckles like an artillery piece. It wobbled erratically. Then she held the cue between thumb and forefinger, but this didn't work either. She tried resting it on the flat of her palm; making a platform of her fingertips; holding it in a loose fist; until by trial and error she found a position novel, yet satisfactory to herself. She was small; bending low was awkward. She poised herself over the table, rump raised, sighting in along the cue. She aimed . . .

"Not enough 'english', Sister."

His voice straightened her small body. The cue, so carefully controlled, flew from her hands crashing against several of the balls on the table and scattering them against the rubber padding, Robert Gerarde laughed aloud.

"Robert! Where did you come from?"

"A little meeting with Mother Prioress. Father Clementi's a far better salesman than I'll ever be. I decided to leave him a clear field." He surveyed the table with an innocent smile, "Private game?"

She overcame her surprise. "We're having our first open house for young people tomorrow; this is the main attraction, we hope."

Robert's eyes took in the three small streamers, the bare walls, the islands of furniture. "This is it? The whole party?"

"I ran out of paper streamers before I ran out of corners. Anyway you can't eat streamers; and we will have plenty of cake and lemonade.

"You giving lessons in the fine art of pocket billiard?"

"That's Father Clementi's job." She eyed Robert mischievously. "But I might give a few lessons in the rhumba, to some of these bashful teenage diamonds in the rough."

Robert threw up his hands in mock horror. "Rhumba! You have to know the Frug and Watusi, and the Monkey and the Slop. You've been out of circulation longer than you think."

"Then I'll learn from them, Robert."

With his help she collapsed the ladder and set it down against a wall. Robert was gently nostalgic rather than sarcastic. "We had bigger parties during lunch hours at the conservatory."

"This will seem just as big here, Robert."

"Lucienne . . ."

"Sister Ann," she hastened to correct him.

"Look, I don't know the protocol, how you're supposed go talk to a nun . . . but you and I knew each other a long time. What made you give up everything?

59

You get up in the middle of the night for a miserable breakfast; you knock yourself out all day; live in this old mausoleum! What kind of girl wants to spend her life like that?"

"Ugh!" She made a face. "Not me."

"Then what in God's name are you doing here?"

"Working . . . in God's name. I 'get up in the middle of the night' to pray. Then I have that 'miserable breakfast,' followed by doing the dishes and Mass; I study, I make visits in the neighborhood, I work with the children . . ." She took in the room with a sweep of her hand, ". . . interior decorating. Even billiards! What more could any girl ask for!"

Robert enjoyed her teasing. But it was precisely what perplexed him. "How can you joke about it?"

"Because I'm happy." She whispered, "I even have a dispensation to laugh . . . as long as I don't overdo it."

She remained an enigma. He apologized for his attitude, the week before at the recording session. It was his custom to listen to every recording made at the studios by an unknown artist. It caused incalculable wear and tear on his eardrums, but once in a while he discovered some real talent this way. Besides he could not get the thought of Lucienne out of his mind, nor the memory of her budding talent at the Conservatory.

"I heard your songs. That's why I'm here."

"Like them?"

"I came to get permission to sign you to a recording contract. Make an album."

"Me!" She thought he was kidding so she teased him back. "You think there's a market for my 'hymns.' "

He winced at the needling, but he was serious. "I'm sure of it. We'll start them out on radio and juke-boxes . . ."

So little was Sister Ann caught up by his suggestion that her mind immediately leaped back to Samaritan House. "Juke boxes." It was a sudden inspiration.

"Stop fooling Robert and be serious. You could get us

a juke box, couldn't you? Rent us one for tonight's dance! . . . Free?"

"Free! That's a nice low rent. Just because you're dedicated to poverty don't think you can drag me along with you. Juke boxes run several thousand dollars. Even at Primavera we don't rear back and pass a miracle every time someone needs a juke box." He was teasing her just as they used to kid each other five years ago.

She accepted the kidding. "We'll play nothing but records made by Primavera. You could supply those, too . . . think of the publicity, Robert."

Robert threw up his arms in surrender. "Hey, easy, easy. One Father Clementi around here is enough!"

One Father Clementi was almost not enough to convince Sister Claire. Despite his careful explanation of the details of the contract, his assurances about the music, and the possibilities that successful records might bring to Samaritan House and to the missions, she hesitated in giving permission. The responsibility was hers. Not only for the reaction that the public might have to a singing nun on records but particularly for the effect that this little fame might have on a young nun. Father Clementi was too wise to omit any argument, too appreciative of her responsibility to attempt to force her to a decision. What he wanted to do was present all of the potential and leave the choice to her.

"It's a good contract, Mother. Both for distribution and the promotion of the album."

"But she's a nun. Singing . . . appearances in front of an audience . . ."

"You've sung in church, Mother; and in front of an entire congregation."

Sister Claire relied heavily on the shrewd and practical advice of Sister Cluny. She knew from experience when Gloomy Cluny was wavering toward a yes or holding staunchly to a no. She seemed to be holding staunchly. "A church is God's house, Father . . ."

"And our royalties were the grace of God," Sister Claire added.

"Sister Ann would still earn those royalties in addition, Mother."

The Prioress wanted to say yes. She liked saying yes. Yet a singing nun, public appearances, promotion, publicity. All these words seemed so foreign that she resisted.

"She's young, inexperienced. There's danger in being in such a spotlight; thrusting her into an atmosphere that's completely alien and certainly not in the tradition of the self-effacing, unworldly nun."

Father Clementi knew she was only hesitating, that she wished to give approval. He was so enthusiastic about the project that he felt no hesitation himself. "Mother, if we can bring our untried young nuns here to live and work side by side with the poor, the suffering, the desperate, surely one of them can endure a press party or singing a few songs in public. The songs deserve to be heard widely; why not let people hear a happy nun singing them?"

Why not?

In the control booth, Robert waved enthusiastically to Sister Ann, then bent over the talk-back microphone by an audio console.

"Bravo! Wonderful, Sister. Wonderful."

It had been a long and tiring day, but both Robert and Sister Ann were very satisfied with the recording session. She sat on a high stool, a microphone lowered to catch her voice from a long-armed boom.

This studio at Primavera Records was a giant step away from the closet in which she had recorded her first songs. It was the first class, "star" studio; heavy velour drapes from floor to ceiling; thick carpeting; acoustical tiled ceiling, all designed to purify the sound of her voice and her guitar. Three weary musicians adding rhythm background mashed out their last cigarettes and hastily packed their instruments to conclude a long day. Sister Mary and Sister Michele, whose voices had been added to enrich the choruses of some of the songs, hurried into the control room as they had done after each recording to see and hear the tape recording being played back by the engineer.

The studio door left open by the departing musicians drew in the echo of their footsteps down the long since emptied halls. Alone in the cavernous studio Sister Ann yawned, slid from her stool rubbing wearied eyes. In one corner of the studio was a grand piano flanked by a large comfortable couch. She sat down on the edge of that, bent her head down to her knees and dangled her fingers down to the carpet flooding her brain and her fingertips with fresh blood, and she hoped, fresh energy.

Father Clementi and the engineer had recognized the professional in each other at the start of this long day. The priest had a quick understanding of the use and importance of the various dials and shared with Robert a mutual zest for perfection which had required take after take after take from the willing nun. Seeing that Sister Ann had settled for a rest, Robert turned to the engineer.

"Why don't you cut a disc while you check the playback. You'd like a copy of everything, wouldn't you, Father?"

Father Clementi had loosened his roman collar in the excitement and the heat of the confining control room, and now his face broke out in a small boy's smile. Would he like a copy! "I was trying to get up the nerve to ask. Thank you Robert."

The engineer coughed. "Want me to sweeten any of the levels, Mr. Gerarde?"

Robert was half-way out of the control booth but turned back to shake a warning finger. "Don't change a decibel. If she sneezed in the middle of a chorus, leave it in."

Sister Mary, appreciating his devotion to detail all day, breathed a mock sigh of exasperation. "The way you have to humor these temperamental, creative people!"

Robert had enjoyed the day not only because the recording session had gone so well but because this, his first association with nuns and a priest on anything but the most formal basis, had developed a surprisingly warm friendship. "That's right Sister. On this album, I am ruthless." He frowned severely. "Absolute dictator!"

"Mr. Gerarde, compared to Mother Prioress and Sister Cluny," Sister Mary called after him, "you're about as much a dictator as Santa Claus."

The two nuns, Father Clementi and the engineer turned to the loudspeaker in the control booth, listening intently to the playback of this final recording, which Robert had approved. Despite the long hours and the repetition, they devoted all their attention to listening for the slightest flaw which might detract from Sister Ann's performance. It was like having four mothers-in-law waiting with loving pride, but every critical sense sharpened, to inspect their first grandchild.

Robert hurried to congratulate Sister Ann and out of habit almost bent down to kiss her cheek in congratulations; but he drew back in time, remembering that this was no recording starlet, but a nun. He took her hand warmly. "Relax a while; no more tonight. You really were wonderful!"

Abruptly he realized the familiarity of even holding her hand and quickly let it go to sit beside her on the couch. "We have enough for a fine album."

"I'm glad." Sister Ann smothered a yawn. "It's fun, but I'm glad."

"Rough day?" he sympathized.

" 'Getting up in the middle of the night' . . . 'miserable breakfast' . . . you know my routine."

"Too much billiards and dancing with those teenagers last night," Robert laughed. He loosened his tie, stretched his legs and leaned back against the comfortable pillows of the couch. "I don't know why I'm tired. You did all the work."

The sound of the playback filtered into the studio through a loudspeaker. But both Sister Ann and Robert were too weary from their work to want to hear the music again. Robert signalled through the glass of the control room for the engineer to turn off their loudspeaker.

"Hungry?"

Convents didn't keep restaurant hours. Sister Ann knew that she had worked straight through her evening meal. Until now she had been too excited, too heavily concentrating on her work, to think of eating. But relaxed, her work done, she needed food.

"Good. I sent out for sandwiches and coffee." He grinned at her. "Five years ago I would have invited you to some cool jazz and a few drinks!"

"Five years ago, Robert, I'd have accepted." She turned to him suddenly laughing. "In fact it seems to me, I did."

"Only five years ago . . ."

Sister Ann rose and began replacing her guitar in its case. They would have to get back to the convent soon, but Robert persuaded her that the food would be delivered very shortly. The other Sisters and Father Clementi must be hungry too. And he decided to supply the music himself; not cool jazz but a deightful comic melody he had written years ago at the Conservatory.

Sister Ann hummed along with it. They laughed over remembered phrases of its lyric. It was amazing, he told her, what a few years did. It gave you perspective, let you see yourself and the world around you much more clearly, made you clear about your own ability so that you could even laugh at yourself. Then he began to play more seriously. Sister Ann listened.

"That's from our musical."

Robert nodded. "Remember it?"

"I'll never forget it." It was the kind of haunting melody that you might momentarily forget but you could always be reminded of.

"Then come on, play it with me."

She hesitated. Then, noting they were still busy in the

control room, she nodded, brought her guitar from its case and sat near him on the piano bench, adding full, rich chords to the simple melody he played. It was a romantic song from a romantic musical play he had composed many years ago. When they finished they were both silent a moment, each caught up in the memories it evoked. Finally Sister Ann turned to him.

"Remember the time you invited me to the jazz concert at the old opera house."

He remembered. The two of them had gone to hear a concert by a visiting American jazz group. The only way he could afford it was by having them both serve as ushers. They had confused tickets for the right aisle with tickets for the left aisle, causing confusion which had delayed the concert by more than 15 minutes. The chaos had been so overwhelming that she couldn't stay annoyed at him for inviting her to a concert and then making her work to hear it. "I didn't promise you tickets," he had declared innocently. "Only the chance to attend." Afterwards they had gone back stage and sat in with some of the musicians, playing through most of the night for the fun of it.

"What a wonderful concert!" Sister Ann recalled.

"Music always spoke a special language to you and me. You've grown musically. You have a whole new dimension you never had then."

"It comes from being happy, Robert."

Robert nodded. He had been listening to that happiness all afternoon and evening in her singing. He lightly plucked the strings of her guitar. "Professor Van Atta would be proud."

Sister Ann stooped over, imitating the almost forgotten music professor from the Conservatory: "Dot guitar, young miss, iss a muzical inzstrumendt; not a defenzive veapon! Do not glutch it to your bosom like a virst born! Do not point it like a machine gun in dose American gangzter vilms! And do not ztrangle it as if it vas . . . this 'beloved' music provessor!"

They laughed together over her takeoff, reliving the rapport they found in music past and present. They had shared many good days, many good times. And each still greatly admired the other's talents.

"You haven't changed," Robert looked at her admiringly. "You really haven't changed at all."

"You have." She was serious now. Honest concern prodded her to seek out the reason why a man of Robert Gerarde's talents had abandoned creative work entirely. "What happened to your music. You had several things almost finished."

He shrugged. "Never got past 'almost.' "

"Why, Robert?"

"Well . . . I just never did. I lacked the discipline. Now I have the discipline but I lack the encouragement; maybe the inspiration that I had."

His meaning was very clear. He looked at her.

"Ah, for the 'good old days' . . . hmmm, Robert?"

"Miss them?"

"I remember them, fondly. I don't really miss them."

"But they were . . . good days."

She admitted that they were. But she reminded him that the older they got the better their memories made them. Five years was a long, long time.

"Not so long." Robert lit a cigarette to keep from looking at her. "I'd say we distilled most of them into these past few hours."

Their probing of each other's emotions was halted by the brisk entrance into the studio of the engineer, with the two nuns and Father Clementi, all following a waiter in white jacket struggling with an enormous covered tray. They hurried to the table where the waiter uncovered his tray, revealing sandwiches, salad, some cold chicken and wine. The engineer nudged Father Clementi to hurry up and say grace. He was starving. The sight of food had suddenly reminded all of them of empty stomachs. As they moved into the studio Robert rose and followed them to the small table returning to his zestful mood.

"An artist dines on beauty and truth! Who needs food?"

"Me!" Sister Ann joined in hurriedly. "You can have all the beauty and truth you find lying around the studio, Robert! I'll take the sandwiches!"

CHAPTER VII

The pendulum of Sister Ann's life began to swing back and forth between two vividly different worlds. There were follow-up recording sessions and a series of conferences to detail the campaign to promote her album of songs. She had to approve each recording, a design for the album cover, and most difficult of all, those descriptive notes without which no self-respecting record album appears willing to present itself to the public. She refused to allow any biographical material about herself: She refused to allow any photographs. So the notes spoke not of Sister Ann but of her songs.

She worried over the money spent and the time squandered in travelling back and forth to Primavera Records. It was not only her own time but the time of another nun, usually Sister Mary, who accompanied her. She apologized to Mother Prioress for the loss of work which her absence represented and frequently discussed what course of conduct she should follow in meetings and conferences with recording and promotion executives of Primavera Records.

Should she for example, eat the lavish spread which typically attended any luncheon meeting? Would it be in keeping with their austere way of life to refuse this food or would it simply draw attention to a display of her nun's vows?

These might seem small problems; yet for a young nun attempting to find a new place, in the world but not of the world, the problems became daily headaches. Nevertheless, she seemed to avoid the pitfalls and each day grew more confident of her ability to function in an atmosphere where glamour and flamboyance, rather than humility and piety, were the touchstones.

At Samaritan House many of her tasks were assumed by the other nuns. None objected; not only because they accepted it without question as their duty, but because each believed that Sister Ann's music was an important contribution in an apostolic way, in addition to being a hope for financial salvation.

The other sisters gave themselves to their varied tasks with the same enthusiasm as Sister Ann gave to her recording work. The work with teenagers, handled largely by Sister Michele and Sister Gertrude, progressed slowly. Each year the children grew older and seemed to harden the shell of sadness and despair into which many of their parents had long since withdrawn. Sister Elise stayed up so late at night learning how to use knitting machines so that she could instruct the women of the neighborhood in method of earning money in their spare time, that she frequently was unable to hold her eyes open at the breakfast table and fell asleep. She was embarrassed when someone woke her, but she was determined to learn and become a good teacher.

Two of the other nuns had begun daily visits in the neighborhood, knocking on doors and greeting whoever lived there with a friendly hello and the offer to help with anything that needed doing, from baby sitting to cleaning house. For the first week they had returned home each day with nothing to show for their generous offers but weary feet and knuckles bruised. But in the second week of their travels they found one family of seven with a mother too ill to take care of her household. She was also too ill to do anything but accept their offers. They had returned to Samaritan House long after ten o'clock at night, exhausted, but rewarded by the knowledge they had made contact with at least one family.

In sharp contrast, Sister Ann, partly for lack of opportunity and partly because she was so busily involved in her work with Primavera Records, had grown no closer to any of the Arliens except Dominic. She determined that she would begin to carry her weight at Samaritan House by learning to assist Sister Mary who was a trained nurse, in a crude clinic which the young African nun had set up in one of the unused rooms. After mastering Sister Mary's instructions in first aid Sister Ann began practicing the use of a hypodermic needle for injections. The usual vaccines were available through the government, but in this neighborhood most had neglected to use this important, free medical service.

In a campaign which Sister Mary claimed she modelled on the eminent success of Father Clementi, the nurse had obtained a sizable store of free supplies from the government. The balance of her equipment came from the Mother House at Bornham. There was a sink, table and chairs in the room. Along one wall she had placed a battered cabinet with sterile bandages and a few simple medicines. Her *piece de resistance,* a gift of a sympathetic doctor in a nearby hospital, was an ancient sterilizer. Thus equipped and prepared Sister Mary now devoted her time to teaching her pupil.

Sister Ann learned how to prepare and lay out a medical tray. It was draped with a cloth and displayed like a classic still life: a potato, a cotton swab, and an empty hypodermic needle.

"It's the only way to learn" Sister Mary insisted. "We had to do it dozens of times in nursing school."

Sister Ann reluctantly lifted the potato from the tray,

took the hypodermic needle in the fingers of her right hand.

"I warn you . . . I faint at the sight of a bloody nose."

Sister Mary was firm. "When you have a hundred screaming children to inoculate in Africa some day you won't have time to faint."

"Listen to Sister Heartless." Sister Ann poised the needle.

"That's me," Sister Mary nodded. "I don't see arms any more, just potatoes."

It was an ancient device for learning, although Sister Mary had explained there was no substitute for true practice on human beings. With heroism beyond the call of duty, she had volunteered to offer her own arm; but first she would have to be satisfied of Sister Ann's control of the needle via the potato. Friendship and dedication, after all, must not exceed reason.

Sister Mary wisely knew that for some people, even the thought of a needle penetrating the hard meat of a potato much less human flesh, was enough to bring nausea. She had mentioned the people in Africa as a further inducement since Sister Ann already was fully aware of the crucial need for inoculation among the many poor people of this neighborhood. Strong motivation, Sister Mary believed, would overcome queasiness.

Sister Ann raised the needle, corrected her fingers in the proper grip, and plunged it roughly into the potato. The needle pierced the skin and penetrated to the hilt.

"If you learned, I'll learn . . . if it kills me."

She tried again, this time no more gently than the first.

"Kills *you?*" Sister Mary made a face. "Those poor, defenseless children!"

The friend's laughter was interrupted by a knock on the door. Sister Elise entered supporting a young woman no more than twenty-two, with the emaciated, aged appearance of malnutrition. She wore a plain, thin dress of a print material, the large figure of which looked gaudy on her small frame.

Jeannette, Sister Elise explained, had fainted in the middle of her knitting class. She left the recovering young woman in their gentle care. Jeannette rose from the chair on still wobbly legs, asserting a belligerence which was as natural to her as breathing. She stared sullenly at the two nuns.

"Can I help you," Sister Mary leaned toward her solicitously.

"This a clinic?"

"That's right." Sister Mary waited; no response. "What can I do for you?"

The woman eyed her a moment, still disdaining to make any response. Making her insult clear, she deliberately moved from the chair, brushed past Sister Mary, and stared at Sister Ann.

"You work here, too?"

The atmosphere in the small room became charged with tension. Both nuns were sharply aware of the insult the woman had made, yet the training of each was to help those who came to this clinic. Sister Mary gestured to her companion to ignore it. She busied herself by replacing the inoculation practice materials in the small cabinet.

"Yes, I'm Sister Ann . . . what do you want?" Sister Ann stood stiffly, unable to conceal her annoyance. They were only trying to help.

"I'm pregnant," Jeannette spoke as if the words were a challenge.

Sister Ann was relieved. She ignored the hard attitude now, the obvious nervousness, mistaking its cause. For her pregnancy was automatically a joyous event, the happy occasion for celebration. Her own nervousness betrayed itself in the effusive congratulations she offered the woman.

"How wonderful . . . your first?" She didn't wait for an answer. "I hope you have a fine healthy baby. Just sit down and make yourself comfortable. There's nothing to worry about. We understand." She found a pencil and paper in the table and sat down to scribble out the information. "What's your name?"

There was no answer. "I need your name and address for the records; we have vitamins for you, monthly check-ups . . . and there's a fine hospital. When your baby's due I'll arrange everything for you."

"I don't want this baby."

Sister Ann stared at her.

"The only thing you can arrange for me, Sister, is an abortion."

Sister Ann was hit hard by the words. In her desire to show friendship and help she ignored what the woman implied from the start, prattling on like a school girl. Now she became righteous, her surprise and shock obscuring good sense and understanding. It was wrong. It was sinful. The words came in a flood. It would be murdering her own child.

Sister Mary interrupted her. In contrast to the wrath of Sister Ann and the savageness of Jeannette, Sister Mary maintained a professional calm.

"Maybe I can help you. I'm the nurse." Jeannette whirled to face her, glaring. Her turmoil was bubbling nearer the surface with every word. She was a human being in the agony of desperation, and in that agony she lashed out most strongly at the very ones whose help she would not admit was her one source of hope.

"You?" she shouted. "Are there different rules for you and her?"

"The rules are the same. For everyone, everywhere." Sister Mary was unruffled; refusing to take offense.

"You won't help me?"

"Our job is keeping people alive. Not killing them. You knew we couldn't help you with an abortion when you came in here."

Jeannette showed the strain in her voice and in her manner. Her face grew paler as she felt herself teetering on the thin edge of control.

"I thought there might be a chance. Just a chance! In

a neighborhood like this maybe you'd understand . . . well I'm the fool. There's never any chance!" Her breath came in short jerking sobs. All she could do now was lash out. "You're here to help us live? Well, 'live' is a funny word, Sister; it has different meanings. For people like you it's easy: you can think of next week, next year. For us it's how to get from today to tomorrow. Just that far. What would you understand, anyway? A black girl from Africa and a nun!"

She stood there breathing heavily. She stared at Sister Mary defiantly, like a small child who has slapped his mother and waits, trembling and yet hoping that a challenge thrown so boldly will somehow solve things.

Sister Ann stood to one side, the shock worn off but not knowing what to do. Abruptly Jeannette dropped her head in her hands and began to sob; convulsive sobs without the release of tears. Sister Ann instinctively started to move between the woman and Sister Mary. But the nurse held out her arm and shook her head gesturing Sister Ann away. She took a pitcher of water from the table and poured some into a glass.

"Drink this." Sister Mary held the glass in front of the woman speaking firmly without emotion. "Go ahead. You'll feel better. Help calm you down."

She took the glass and held Jeannette's hands to its sides. The woman swallowed several gulps of cool water. Then Sister Mary sat beside her, speaking calmly and matter of factly.

"No more tears now, hmm? I know what you are going through. I was born in a mud shack with a tin roof in a village without food or sanitation or medicine. My mother didn't want a baby . . . she already had borne four others and none of them got from 'today to tomorrow' for as long as six months. So, when she realized she was carrying me, my mother went to the medicine man; for the same reason you came here. He was willing . . . so they tried. Spells, magic potions, heaven knows what 'medicines' he concocted; my mother tried them all."

The woman had lifted her head. The sobs stopped. She was drawn into Sister Mary's story because the nun told it not with self-pity nor exaggeration but in the awareness that she offered understanding built on a firm foundation of common experience. Sister Ann, her emotions torn by her own reactions, by the plight of the woman, and by her awareness of the difference between her own approach and Sister Mary's, listened carefully as her sister nun continued.

"But every day of my life since I was old enough to understand what they tried, I prayed my thanks, that nothing worked. You called me a 'black girl from Africa and a nun.' I'm both of those. And proud of it. I've tried to make my life very special and devote it to doing something worth while." Sister Mary looked at the woman, their faces close now, and added something very softly. "I believe that I am."

"I'm . . . I'm sorry I said that. I'm falling apart . . . the baby's father, he . . . I don't even know where he is any more. What am I going to do?"

"I'll help you. If you can't come here I'll go to you. We'll pray together. Things work out."

Sister Mary rose and opened the cabinet. Sister Ann took her handkerchief and wiped away the woman's tears. Then smiling she dabbed at her own with the same cloth: "I'll stop if you stop . . ."

The woman was revived by the catharsis of tears. She managed a small smile at Sister Ann: "You first."

Sister Mary returned from the cabinet bearing a small bottle of vitamins.

"Right now I'd suggest you go home and get some rest. Start taking these every morning. I'll come by sometime later this afternoon and we can discuss things a little further." She smiled. "You don't feel like talking any more now."

The woman nodded, gratefully accepted the vitamins and left. Sister Mary closed the door behind her and stood there to take a deep breath. She too, had been moved.

Sister Ann sat at the table frustrated by her ineptness. When would she learn? Or was she simply and clearly a round peg in a square hole? She failed not as a nurse, but as a human being and particularly as a nun. Instead of love she had offered reproach; instead of patient understanding she had reacted with naivete.

"Compared with the way I bungled *that* I'm a whiz with potatoes." She toyed with the hypodermic needle, seeking to understand herself.

"I've had a lot more experience; I grew up like her. Just be friendly. A neighbor."

Sister Ann looked straight at her fellow nun. They were friends: she wanted her to be tough, to examine Sister Ann and give a good clinical report.

"You're attacking problems. They aren't problems; they're people."

Sister Ann nodded. "She was like Mr. Arlien. They all have a . . . a suit of armor around them. I don't get through."

"When people build barriers of hate and fear around themselves like that, the only thing that can penetrate is love."

It seemed a peculiar weapon to Sister Ann. "They seem so hard. Full of hate."

"You have to be taught to hate, Sister. And they have." Sister Mary spoke softly but her words reflected the feeling within her, an awareness of other human beings so strong that each seemed as close to her as a member of her family. She watched Sister Ann trying to absorb her words. She knew hatred seemed an impossible thing to explain to the young nun. "But the opposite of love isn't hate, its indifference; and I think that's worse, don't you?"

The two nuns, one infected with love for her fellow human beings, the other suffering the wounds of self-doubt sat together in silence and thought and prayed in that sterile room.

CHAPTER VIII

Like an endless series of black whirlpools, the pressing machine stamped out the records with spiraling lines of sound: each identical, each identified at the vortex with the simple label "The Singing Nun." They were produced first in the plant at Primavera Records, then as the demand grew other plants were licensed to produce them, too. A complex network of distribution and merchandising was tied together and the campaign launched with an efficiency matching the invasion of D-day. The success of the records was far swifter than any invasion.

Young people danced to them. Children clapped their hands. Old folks hummed; and cash registers smiled the loudest. The first recording of "The Singing Nun" was, in the jargon of the business, "a smash."

In contrast to the feeling of failure which Sister Ann had as a nun, was the total success which Robert Gerarde and his fellow executives discussed in the elegant conference room of Primavera Records. They had all heard the pressings of the nun's songs. The question was how properly to merchandise them; how to balloon a success into a spectacular new star. At first they assumed that this was something for the specialty market; unique, a rarity, a freak. But Robert convinced them that they had a sleeper. The songs were good, they had the simplicity for wide appeal. The key was exploitation. A few appearances before selected groups of publicity people; a performance here and there . . . just enough to whet the appetite, but with an air of the exotic. He had the entire campaign in mind. And the nun herself? He knew her personally, knew her well. She'd draw fans and attention as a flame draws moths!

Sister Ann's life entered a new and dizzying phase. She was pulled in two directions; excited and pleased by the success of the campaign on which Robert led her, while simultaneously frustrated by a succession of failures in her work at the convent. It was a relief that the pressures of her recording efforts pre-empted most of her time.

The promotional appearances began one day at an elegant garden party which took place at the home of Mr. Duvries. It was a sparkling afternoon and the brightness of the day vied with the bubbling guests. Small tables leap frogged across the lawn under brightly striped canvas umbrellas; regiments of flowers were on dress parade; laughter tinkled; corks popped; waiters scurried; an orchestra discretely serenaded.

At the rear of the high-walled yard a small decorated pavilion, raised two steps from the yard level, provided a stage. Attending the party were a noisy, well-dressed, sophisticated group as individual as a modern artist's collage. There were about equal parts publicity people and columnists, music reviewers and personalities and social friends of Robert's and Mr. Duvries who fell into the category of "taste-maker." All agreed it was a wonderful party; all wanted to know who it was for.

"You know Robert: always business with pleasure. We're to witness a debut. Discovery of his."

A thin man made a face over the rim of his champagne glass.

"Wants a feature in my magazine about her."

"Well, he better hurry up and trot her out." The sleek woman behind him raised her glass. "Or half the guests are going to get stoned on this champagne."

"If she's anything like the 'talent' I heard at the last discovery party I went to, you'll wish you were!"

On a sunporch at the back of the house Sister Ann had been waiting nervously with Father Clementi and Sister Cluny. Robert approached her, all confidence.

"Ready?"

Sister Ann gripped her guitar tightly. "I guess so . . ."

She followed him through the door of the sunporch toward the small pavilion.

"Don't be nervous," whispered Father Clementi.

"I'm not," she replied. "I'm petrified."

"I'll be right here behind you, rooting for you."

Sister Ann's throat was dry and her fingertips perspiring but she managed a small smile. "Father . . . have *you* ever thought of taking up singing?"

Robert had seized the moment and stepped out onto the small stage, lifting his hand to quell the applause.

"Ladies and gentlemen of the press, distinguished guests, friends. Thank you all for coming today. This party is my way of making an introduction on behalf of Primavera Records. I would like you to meet a young lady with a pleasant voice and a delightful way with her guitar. The songs are her own: music from the heart; feeling from the soul . . . of The Singing Nun . . ." He gestured her out. "Sister Ann!"

There was polite applause. She stepped onto the platform and shyly sought a comfortable place on the high stool which had been placed there for her. In the crowd, eyebrows and eyes were raised in gruesome expectation. It was true: a nun. As they watched her settling, they prepared themselves for the pain to come. They smothered yawns, suppressed laughter, a few found ears to scratch, a nose that needed powdering, eyes to be improved with glasses. Many regretted that they had failed to refill their glasses.

Her fingers trembled a little with nervousness; she clapped them across the strings to gain control, acknowledged the crowd with a bob of the head, and with a deep breath, began. It was a shock. No thin-voiced, shrill, pious hymn singing: no. With all the verve and joy that was at the heart of her music she began to entertain them.

After the first verse she was at home and began to move freely, working instinctively to her audience. The lyrics and the lilting melody she communicated with such unexpected warmth and skill that it was but a few moments before she had captured them. They were hers. The show business cynics, the criticial reviewers, the bored publicity people and columnists, the inattentive "taste-makers," surrendered unconditionally. Father Clementi nodded his head and hummed quietly from the beginning. Sister Cluny tapped a toe carefully hidden by her skirt.

Robert Gerarde, instead of surveying the reaction of this audience, face by face, could not keep his eyes away from Sister Ann.

Her enjoyment of the music was infectious. When she finished the crowd was in a half circle around her applauding and cheering with enthusiastic delight. She hesitated a moment, accepting the applause with pleasure, but not knowing how to get off the stage gracefully. Robert moved quickly to her side. Unable to stifle the applause he whispered, "Congratulations," to her. Finally there was quiet.

"Ladies and gentlemen, would you like to hear more of Sister Ann?"

The crowd responded with resounding affirmatives.

"I thought you would," Robert smiled, "So I've arranged for you to hear lots more; on Primavera Records, of course!"

There was good natured laughter as he pointed to a multi-tiered display rack of her album which was being brought out from the house.

"Complimentary albums for each of you, and a buffet inside. And a chance for you to meet Sister so you can write your reviews with a personal touch."

As he shepherded her back to the sunporch Father Clementi came to congratulate her.

"Wonderful, Sister, wonderful . . . I wanted to hear a lot more too."

"I think I might be able to find an extra album for you Father," Robert offered innocently. "I'll even let you have it for the wholesale price."

The second surprise was her interview. Sister Ann was modest but like most artists she shone under the stimulus of approval. She was a gregarious happy person: that was the foundation for her songs and for the way she blossomed now. When she had satisfied their curiosity and assured them that she was, indeed, a Dominican nun, they began to question her about her music. The songs, they all agreed, were lovely. A unique combination of prayer and simple folk music that made each more meaningful by the combination. But how did she happen to find that happy connection.

"I imagine God may get tired of our formal traditional praying once in a while, don't you? It's easy to want to find something new; to express it in a modern manner and still have meaning is not so easy. If you'll bear with me for a story perhaps I can explain. While I was still a novice at the convent we were assigned to teach religion each week to a group of Irish children at an orphanage nearby. One day at Mass I was quietly explaining and encouraging a prayerful attitude toward this great worship of our faith. I told this little Jimmy . . . whispering, of course, in the hushed church . . . to watch as the priest raised the sacred chalice and then to pray humbly to himself: 'My Jesus, Mercy!'" She whispered now, "Jimmy nodded enthusiastically as I illustrated for him. The next day, again at Mass, Jimmy nudged me and smiled knowingly as this part approached. There's nothing quite so endearing as the innocent enthusiasm of a six-year-old boy to something you yourself have taught him. The priest raised the sacred chalice, and in a stage whisper penetrating the farthest corner of the reverent silence in the church . . . as only the 'whisper' of a small boy can . . . the entire congregation was edified to hear my Jimmy's devoted prayer: 'My Jesus . . . *Murphy*'!"

She drew a warm hearty laugh. When it abated she added

"He taught me something, that Jimmy. And I hope it answers your question: simple, meaningful communication is as necessary when we pray as any other time."

That night, for the first time since she had discovered Nicole's photographs and been forcibly ejected from the Arlien household, Sister Ann returned. She walked down the street carrying a large paper sack but as she approached the door she stopped and stared at the Arlien house remembering her last visit and the warning from Mr. Arlien. She was not afraid; she simply wished to respect his wishes. Instead of knocking she turned, found a side alley and walked down it toward the rear of the house. The alley emptied into a cluttered rear yard, and reaching it she noticed a small figure stepping out of the back door adjusting a black eyepatch, pirate style, over his eye.

"Dominic?"

He whirled, ever alert; but noting her white robes he broke out into a big smile. "Hi!"

She moved to him, holding out the paper sack, warmed by knowing that her absence had not lost the small boy's friendship.

"What's in there, Sister?"

"A few things from a party I went to."

Dominic Arlien had been to three parties in his lifetime. At the first when he was three or four, he couldn't remember which, there had been a cake with candles and of distant relatives and forgotten friends all encouraging him to blow, make a wish, and be happy. The second party was a memory that was sharp. His father had lost his job and come home to "celebrate" with them. He was drunk. It was a strange party for himself, Nicole and his father in which, even at his tender age, he could easily see the lack of gaiety behind the smiles and the laughter of the other two.

The third party was only six months ago. A man . . . he did not even know his name, much less his face . . . had died; receiving an unlooked for legacy his heirs had decided on a full-fledged wake. Dominic had been walking down the street when the sounds of laughter and glasses clinking drew him to the windows. To his surprise he was invited inside. To his even greater surprise he noted the gaudy casket in a room adjacent to a table overflowing with good things to eat. These strangers had invited him, in fact urged him strongly, to eat and drink. After eating, the little boy had wandered alone into the adjacent room. The casket was open and he could see the stiff waxen figure that lay inside. He realized then that the celebration was for the dead man and without explanation he came to his own conclusions: life was so miserable that it was a wise thing to celebrate its conclusion.

One thing stood out clearly: regardless of what occasioned parties, they were always accompanied by good things to eat. So, seeing the bulging paper sack, Dominic eagerly invited the nun inside.

"I don't think your father would want me to."

"You and him had a fight or something, huh?"

"A misunderstanding." Sister Ann hesitated, "Is he home?"

Dominic shook his head, "no." "Just me."

"I'd like to apologize. But I don't think I'd better come in unless he invites me."

Dominic was sufficiently aware of the inscrutable ways of adults to ask no questions. His mind skipped ahead to the thing which had occupied it when he came out the door.

"Can you keep a secret?"

Sister Ann assured him that she could.

"I got a hideout. A secret hideout." Dom was very conspiratorial. "Nobody knows except Nicole and papa. Nobody in the whole world!"

"I always wished I had a hideout."

"You got to promise not to tell anybody. Ever. Promise?"

"Promise."

Dom accepted her word. He turned back into the house beckoning for her to follow. Sister Ann came to the doorway but she felt she couldn't go in and stopped at the threshold; waiting for him. The boy moved to the window sill on which rested a cheap glass ball with a scene inside . . . the kind that snows when turned upside down. He peered out the window, then he turned the glass ball and the snow fell.

"That's our signal I'm at the hideout."

"Nicole's a conspirator, too?"

Sister Ann did not talk down to the little boy. She assumed the same grave air of espionage.

"No, Sister. But this way she knows where to find me . . . to help with the dishes or something."

Out into the alley walled by the bleak buildings, they proceeded to a rendezvous with Dom's hideout. The boy closed the door carefully, surveyed the empty yard before them with studied unconcern. He beckoned her to follow him.

"Case anybody's watching . . . ," he whispered, "try not to let 'em notice you."

Sister Ann had been playing the game. It was good therapy for a busy, troubled adult to immerse herself in that simple child's make-believe in which the sole frustration was a lack of imagination. She almost laughed, visualizing some imaginary villain spying on them but not noticing a woman in flowing white robes crossing a small dingy yard.

Single file, across alley and yard, she followed his every footstep: pausing when he paused; glancing about for hidden spies when he looked about, darting into recesses and shadows wherever he led. Of course, anyone but a blind man could have seen them from a thousand yards away, and noting their behavior could have followed them with ease: but that was the game. You pretended that your life depended on secrecy. You imagined that within each shadow and behind every pile of debris waited nameless, formless enemies: otherwise you might as well walk straight across the yard.

Bordering one side of the yard to their left was the drab warehouse wall which cut off the descending sun's light and cast heavy shadows. The warehouse sagged with neglect, its face a stranger to paint or repair for many years. At the rear of the yard where a fence met and made a corner with the warehouse, lay an enormous old wooden shipping crate. Sister Ann looked about wondering where they would go now: over it, or around it. But Dom glanced around, then feeling safe, suddenly lifted the side of the crate. The crate, hinged at the top, swung up and out to allow entrance. Dominic disappeared inside and, astonished by this concealed door, Sister Ann followed.

CHAPTER IX

The crate itself was about an eight foot cube; empty, dirty, but a perfect cover for what it concealed. It lay up against a door, probably the rear entrance to the unused warehouse. Stooping down and crawling along the bottom of the crate behind Dominic, Sister Ann saw the boy push open the bottom half of the old warehouse door, which had been sawed away like the lower half of a dutch door, thereby allowing a hidden access to the building itself. It was indeed a perfect hideout. Sister Ann crawled ahead and rose, finding herself inside the deserted warehouse. Through windows dark with years of neglect, came a dim light.

"Is it safe here?" she whispered.

"Sure." Dom saw no need for whispering any longer. He pointed now and spoke aloud. "Papa fixed it. We don't have any Grandma or Grandpa to go and be with; so he made me this place to visit. Nobody knows about it: I think even Papa maybe forgot its here."

He indicated a flight of stairs leading to the second floor. She followed him. When they reached the top, Sister Ann looked about her in pleased surprise. It was a small room, open to the stairs, empty except for a few left over tools, and old papers in one corner. But it offered a spectacular view over this part of the city, particularly the nearby river, from the only clean window in the room. The floor had been swept and a broken bench propped up with bricks served as a place to sit. She was touched.

"I never had grandparents to visit either, Dominic . . . but this is better. Much better."

By the route Sister Ann had used earlier, Nicole now appeared tracing the same approach, first along the alley then toward the rear door of her house. She was dressed simply again in a sweater and skirt, her hair falling loose and tied with a single ribbon in back. The absence of heavy makeup revealed wan and sunken cheeks, darkening hollows underneath tired eyes, and lips which no longer curled upward but fell in a joyless arc. Even her defiance had fallen away exposing the lonely little girl that she was. Nicole sat on the rear step. She took a battered harmonica from her pocket and began to play. It was a mournful tune: slow, soft, the kind of keening some women sing in mourning. This girl played, staring at the bleak friendless walls of the buildings around her.

Loneliness was the only echo she heard. Some years back a social worker interviewing Nicole Arlien, had noted on her report that the young girl had managed to achieve a remarkable maturity. She had in the words which appeared on the printed form, "adjusted to her environment remarkably well." Any fool could have read in Nicole's eyes the contradiction to those words: unless you would consider a patient as having "adjusted to her environment" when strapped into a hospital bed and injected with a sedative. Nicole Arlien had not adjusted; she had only stopped struggling. Her father's inability to find and hold a job strapped her firmly to her home; a deep and pervasive love for her brother and for her father, too, was the sedative which numbed the cries of despair. She had found a way to keep them going in the only way she could; a way which she knew was demeaning, a solution which stripped away the final tatters of dignity that had cloaked her loneliness.

Nicole played her harmonica, a sad tune from a sad girl. Shifting to a more comfortable position, she stopped abruptly, staring at something that attracted her attention at the house. In the rear window smiling down at her was Dominic's signal. It's grains of plastic snow still plunging through the heavy liquid in the glass sphere. She sat up. She needed company. She smiled as she rose and quickly crossed toward the packing crate in the rear corner of the yard.

In the hideout room upstairs the paper sack Sister Ann brought from the garden party had been emptied on a small table. At either side of it, the nun and the small boy sat pouring over this collection of treasures: a souvenir decoration made with a small plastic record; some salted nuts; candy; a single enormous red carnation; four sandwiches; an orange; and in a paper plate, the jewel in this crown of glories, a large piece of cake.

"We could have our own party," Dominic was enthusiastic.

"Let's."

Dominic touched the riches, unbelieving. The mere touch of things brought such a glow to his eyes that Sister Ann was rewarded.

"I had so much candy once I got sick . . ." he looked at her and then prompted by the urge to honesty in the face of such magnificence he added sheepishly, "I took it from a man who had a cart. When he wasn't looking."

"That was stealing, Dominic." The nun felt she had to add this reminder, more for the sake of form and fulfilling what the boy expected of her than because he needed it.

"I know." The boy was ashamed but forthright. Suddenly he was assailed by a nagging doubt. He looked at her, then at the candy, then back to her. "Sister . . ." he struggled with a decision, then stumbled ahead, "How did *you* get hold of all of this?"

"It was left over, Dominic." The boy nodded, but he glanced away. Such explanations commonly concealed a lie. Some of his joy evaporated but he would not deny this new friend the pleasure of ill-gotten gains. Sister Ann tapped him on the shoulder and assured him: "They gave it to me."

"Well, you can take it right back, Sister!" Nicole's voice cracked like a whip in that quiet room.

She stood in the doorway, angry, hurt and jealous that Dom would share their secret with this intruder. Sister Ann and Dominic whirled to face her. Nicole was no longer listless; she was hard and bitter. Between sister and brother was a fierce affection. The girl resisted help and tried to protect the boy from an involvement with things he could not yet comprehend: things like the lure of a smiling woman who sang songs and brought unheard of riches to tempt him. The prize now was not the gifts scattered on the table top, but the loyalty of a small boy.

"It's real candy, Nicole! And nuts."

Sister Ann had not seen Nicole Arlien since that time, when she had seen her posed naked in the photographs. It was an awkward encounter yet one which the nun had known must come. She had hoped it would be under different circumstances; at a time when the two of them could calmly and dispassionately discuss the girl's future. She recognized that there was a history of hostility being built here. Not only the pages of the past, but her presence here in the secret hideout, the private province of Nicole and her brother, affronted this girl.

How could she say that her heart went out to the Arliens? How could she explain that Dominic had brought her here before she realized what a confidence he was bestowing? How could she give herself to a girl whose defenses were made of steel?

"I thought I'd share these things with you, Nicole.

They were left over from a party I attended this afternoon. Try some?"

"I don't want to share anything of yours."

"Won't you let me be your friend?"

The word friend was particularly odious to Nicole. It grated her nerves and rubbed salt in the wounds of injured trust. The photographer had said he would be her friend. The social worker wanted to be her friend. The obsequious man who called with lewd proposals claimed he was the photographer's friend. The woman who had stolen her grocery money as a child had presented herself as a friend. The policeman who threatened to arrest her called himself her friend. The landlord who now pressured for his rent money on the first of every month had formerly claimed to be her father's friend. The cafe owner who had brought her her father's unpaid bills had represented herself as the family's friend. She hated the word.

"There are only three people in my world. Me, and my father and Dom."

"And me?"

"There's no room for you."

Nicole crossed the room and sat on the bench. Dominic looked from the party things before him to his sister and then back to the nun. The boy was caught in the middle and he could not understand. Why was it that people he liked had to be enemies? Why was it that things he wanted must be the stakes in a game in which he must be only a loser? Was that the lesson that he must learn when his father rambled on and cursed late at night?

Yet despair is an alien feeling in a six year old boy. "She . . . she's nice, Nicole. She brought this . . . and maybe next time she'll play her guitar for us."

Nicole shushed her brother. "There's not going to be a next time. Take your stuff, Sister; we don't want it."

Fear rose in Sister Ann. Not a fear of physical attack but a far deeper fear that these young people she wanted to help, and particularly this girl she wanted to love, were about to fly away from her in anger. She begged Nicole to stay calm and asked her what made her so bitter.

"That's a bright question!" Nicole stood in front of the nun to confront her directly. "You showed those pictures of me to my father. You know damn well, that's why I'm bitter!"

The girl turned away and busied herself with picking up a few things: a plate, a cup, an empty pint gin bottle with a candle. It was a way of gaining control of her temper. Sister Ann hesitated, glanced at Dominic who was watching the conflict between his two friends with a deep frown. She did not want to open questions to which the boy would demand answers, yet she must continue. It was not a matter of pride. It was necessity. She moved closer to Nicole.

"You shouldn't have made those pictures." Her tone was gentle yet there was a command in her voice.

"We have to eat, Sister. Maybe I don't bring home candy, but we do eat!"

"I think your father would rather go hungry, Nicole."

"Do you think I told him where the money came from? What kind of a monster do you think I am? All he knew was that I earned money for food; that's all. I made lots of those pictures, Sister. They bought what went in our bellies or we'd have starved. And once in a while I could buy him a bottle of gin so he wouldn't shake to death from needing a drink. That may not sound nice and clean to you, Sister; that may not sound sweet and lovely; that may not sound pure and religious; it's just true." She glared at the nun. "He still wouldn't know if you hadn't opened your big mouth!"

She began remembering the moment of deep pain between her and her father. It broke her anger and began an avalanche of emotion. "I thought he was going to hit me. My poor father never raised his hand to me in his life before. Ever. I could hear him in the room later. He was crying. My father, crying."

There was a long silence before Sister Ann could bring

herself to answer. She had learned more in those few phrases from a distraught girl than she ever could have been taught in years of classes.

"There are other kinds of work you could try . . ." her voice trailed off, unconvinced.

"I'm too young; or not enough school. My father and me, we're alike." She held the empty bottle tenderly as if through it she could talk to him. "Once he went out looking and looking and looking. They told him they have machines now and the machines do things better and cheaper than he can. Imagine: machines. That made him feel just great! Him, 48 years old, worked like a slave all his life, and now they have a machine!" She thrust her face directly in front of Sister Ann. It was a shout of passion. "So you had to come and show him those damn pictures!"

"Nicole . . . I'm sorry . . ."

"At least while he thought I was working papa could keep on believing that somebody would need him sometime."

Nicole held herself in, tightly controlled. She returned the party things to the sack in which Sister Ann had brought them, and put her arm around Dom protectively. The boy looked up at her in wonder and sympathy. He sensed from her attitude that his sister felt she was very right in scolding Sister Ann. He gave her a smile.

"Why don't you get out of here, Sister? What do you want anyway?"

"Nothing." Sister Ann desperately sought the right approach, the right words. "Nothing . . . except to help you."

"Nobody does something . . . 'for nothing.' "

"You're wrong, Nicole. I want you to see we're part of the same family. God's family. All of us."

"God! You think I still believe in that? Where's that God of yours been hiding all these years?"

"Don't blame Him for the failures of people like me. I admit I don't know much about how you live . . ."

"I'm seventeen." Nicole broke in bluntly. "I'm no holy virgin, Sister. I've been around." Her voice became tough. "Nobody in this manure-pile world gives a damn about me. Unless they want something. Like pictures, Sister, for that they pay money." She took the sack of party things and thrust them hard, directly into Sister Ann's hands. "So don't try to buy me, for a few pieces of candy!"

There was genuine passion beneath the hard words and the suppressed self-pity. Dom, seeing his sister close to tears, turned to stare accusingly at Sister Ann. She stood there as if struck in the face: but the hurt went much deeper. She started to speak, but no words came. Clutching the bag of party things which she hoped might have provided a bridge between her and the Arliens, Sister Ann turned to the stairs and retreated from their hideout and their friendship. What could she say or do?

Early evening shadows chased a warm breeze past Sister Ann as she entered the big door of Samaritan House. Her movements were slow, dejected; unusual for her. She started across the small hall, past the open door of the recreation room toward the kitchen. A voice hissed out at her.

"Sister! Look!"

Sister Michele stood in the doorway to the recreation room. Having gained her audience's attention, she started to juggle three small apples, excited delight danced over her face.

"How's this for a beginner?"

"Not bad," Sister Ann admired.

"I promised some of those little urchins I'd teach them to juggle," Sister Michele explained. "But I had to teach myself first. I started with billiard balls." She made a wry face. "But I dropped one on my foot. It was very discouraging. I kept wondering what excuse I was going to give them each day; but better a lame excuse tham a lame nun, I figured . . . until I saw these apples in the kitchen. They're just right."

She stopped her juggling, breathed a sigh of satisfaction with her progress and held one out.

"Apple?"

"No thanks." Sister Ann appraised her companion's sparkling mood. "You're in awfully good spirits after a long afternoon on duty in the playground!"

"I feel good." Sister Michele beamed. "I signed up fourteen pupils for my nutrition class tonight."

Sister Ann was suitably impressed. "Congratulations . . . that's really making contact. Fourteen!"

"Well . . ." Sister Michele admitted sheepishly, "Three young wives, six mothers, and five kids to eat up all the homework! Sure you won't have an apple?"

Sister Ann shook her head and moved off toward the kitchen. Sister Michele returned to the recreation room biting into one apple and juggling the remaining two with increasing dexterity.

A pot simmered on the kitchen stove. In the center of the room was a large work table on which a series of papers were laid out in very neat bundles: bills, correspondence, reports. The kitchen was Sister Cluny's domain. She was cook, chief maid, and used the kitchen work table as a desk for this staggering mass of paperwork required to run a convent and a household. Sister Ann did not see her as she entered, absorbed in her own thoughts. She took a glass from a counter and moved toward the sink, automatically reaching out to turn on the faucet, Sister Ann paused with hand in mid-air, staring in astonishment. Suspended over the long old-fashioned tap, was a large, black, nun's shoe, gleaming from a fresh shine.

"You can't have a drink yet," Sister Cluny's voice came sharply from the floor behind the work table. She rose bearing two armloads of shoes, a shoe cloth and polish. Dumping them on the floor near the sink Sister Cluny grabbed the shoe on the faucet.

"That's your shoe support? Just like a bootblack isn't it," Sister Ann admired.

"Ummhm" Sister Cluny removed the freshly shined shoe and indicated the faucet. "Go ahead. Drink."

Sister Ann turned on the water and filled her glass, watching the other nun drop to her knees on the floor, spreading out the pairs of shoes in an assembly line for her polish.

"Sit down there. Might as well do yours, too. They're dirty." Sister Cluny barely glanced up as she directed Sister Ann to a nearby chair.

"No, let me help you."

"You'd get in my way. Go sit down."

Sister Ann hesitated. But Sister Cluny had a forceful personality and she spoke in tones of such authority that young nuns hurried to obey. Priests and Prioresses and even Bishops had been known to nod affirmatively at Sister Cluny's command. Perhaps it was because they did not know her well.

At this moment, Sister Ann's will had been reduced to water by her recent experience. She sat down, dejected, admiring the neat papers on the table. Sister Cluny methodically moved from one pair of shoes to the next, working and talking simultaneously.

Her first step was removing dust with a brush. Without turning, without seeming to notice the young nun behind her Sister Cluny warned sharply:

"Don't mess up my papers, please."

Sister Ann straightened up in her chair making certain the sleeves of her cloak would not disturb the orderly piles. She made a little face of approval seeing the organization involved and the amount of work.

"You're the most organized person I ever met, Sister Cluny."

"I already agreed to do your shoes, Sister." Sister Cluny's tone was dry.

"I mean it. Sister Claire would be lost without you; and so would we."

Like many gruff people, Sister Cluny ignored compliments and open affection; they penetrated too deeply.

Her attention moved now to Sister Ann's foot which she lifted in one hand as she brushed the shoe free of dust.

"What do you do, rub these on sandpaper?" Sister Cluny pursed her lips in a familiar sour appraisal. "My budget says you don't get new ones for another three months."

"If I don't do any better than I have . . . I won't be here in three months. Sister Michele's nutrition classes and Sister Elise's sewing group are a terrific success. And Sister Mary with the clinic; you with all the administrative work . . ."

"Feeling awfully sorry for yourself," the older nun interrupted coolly, "Aren't you, Sister?"

"I can't seem to do anything right."

"We had a letter this morning." Sister Cluny found the polish and a dauber. "According to Mr. Gerarde, your record album's going to make lots of money!"

"I need more than money for the Arlien family. Or any of the others." Sister Ann leaned forward with passion. "I want to help them. *Really* help."

Sister Cluny knelt beside her reaching for her foot. She spoke now, very bluntly, without a trace of self-pity.

"When I was your age I wanted to work in an orphanage. All those sweet, innocent, motherless, little babies. Give me your foot, Sister."

"Wait. I'll take them off."

"Give me your foot. It's easier to do them on you."

Over her protest Sister Cluny took Sister Ann's foot, rested it on her own knee, and began polishing.

"The truth is I find it difficult to love a girl like Nicole. I want to do so much . . . but I can't get anywhere with her."

"Don't expect great victories, Sister. Small things only; here, and in the missions. A heart opened; a sacrifice made; a soul turned back to its Maker. Be ambitious for those small victories."

Sister Ann waited a moment before she continued. "You don't feel sorry for yourself, do you, Sister Cluny?"

Sister Cluny continued with the shoes; a deliberately humble task but one which successfully hid her face from Sister Ann. Sister Ann felt uncomfortable at being served. Yet she eagerly wanted to hear more.

"Sister Cluny? . . . You mean 'Gloomy Cluny,' don't you?" She didn't wait for an answer. "No; I don't feel sorry for myself. But I got the name when I was transferred from the orphanage where I was first assigned. After just a few weeks with all those lovely children . . ." her voice trailed off, then resumed, "I'm . . . inept with people, Sister. In my first few years as a nun I discovered I have no particular . . . natural gifts. So I taught myself administration, organization. All those tiresome little details that have no value in themselves but are necessary to make things work. Including a convent." She looked up at Sister Ann. "You may not think so, but I'm very, very happy. Serving Our Lord means doing what He needs; not what we want. The motive is what's important."

"Serving our Lord . . ."

Sister Cluny nodded. "Even in polishing shoes, Sister."

She finished and looked up at her with what was for Sister Cluny a big smile. It was a very warm moment of understanding between these two women, totally different, yet united. Sister Ann smiled back.

"Thank you . . . Gloomy Cluny."

CHAPTER X

"Electricity, Mother." Sister Cluny handed the Prioress the last of a neat stack of bills for which Sister Claire wrote checks. She winced at the figure. "We're going to have to turn the lights out earlier!"

The Prioress nodded assent. "There seems to be an immutable law about bills; no matter what you do or what you stop spending, the bills get larger . . . all by themselves."

There were sacks of mail from the post office and overflowing baskets of answers to those letters which the Prioress had been able to answer. Her office, usually so neat, was in turmoil. Sister Cluny pointed to the sacks.

"Should I send these back to the post office?"

"I never in my wildest dreams imagined there would be all this. Over a record!"

"We can't read it all, Mother. What's the point anyway? They write: 'Dear Sister, We love your album' . . . only it takes most of them a page of two to say it!"

Sister Cluny's heart rebelled at all these words. If you liked something, come out and say it. Don't waste words.

Don't waste paper and particularly don't waste her time reading something which could be said in one sentence. As the two nuns contemplated the unopened mail the bell rang.

"More mail, no doubt." Sister Cluny went to answer.

It was not the postman. A man stood in the doorway; well dressed, with an air of authority, yet in deference to the surroundings in which he found himself. Behind him at the curb Sister Cluny could see his chauffeur driven limousine, already attracting stares from the neighborhood. A rich man in this neighborhood was a rarity; an American, the cause of true curiosity; and had they known that it was Ed Sullivan, himself, the children and teenagers would have come swarming over to him and engulfed the entrance, Samaritan House or no Samaritan House. Sister Cluny opened the door. The man raised his hat.

"Good morning, Sister. I'm Ed Sullivan."

"Good morning . . ." Sister Cluny didn't recognize the name. If she had, she would have said exactly the same thing and reacted in exactly the same way.

"May I come in?"

"What for?"

"Isn't the Prioress expecting me?"

Mr. Sullivan was accustomed to warm welcomes. He was well known. He was among the top men in his field. Appearances on his show were like invitations to a command performance. Most of those who received requests leaped at the chance. He was a master at the hard-bitten negotiating which is the business side of Show Business. He was also a genial man with a thousand friends and uncounted acquaintances. He was accustomed to smiles as well as welcomes. What faced him now was a nun, staring at him with all the warmth he could expect if he had just informed her he was about to burn down the convent. For perhaps the first time in Ed Sullivan's life he was without words.

"Didn't you get my letter?" he finally managed.

"Probably. We haven't had time to open them all."

"I asked for an appointment to discuss Sister Ann . . . didn't you open the Cardinal's letter either?"

The name Ed Sullivan might not open doors: the word Cardinal did.

"You might as well come in. This way, please."

The Prioress welcomed Ed Sullivan. She apologized about his letter and about the Cardinal's. Though she did not recognize his name, knew nothing of his pre-eminence in his field, she recognized that a man with an introduction from the Cardinal deserved to be listened to. By way of apology she showed him Samaritan House. Now she sat at her desk listening to him; Sister Cluny stood like a bulldog near the sacks of mail. Ed Sullivan, beginning to warm to his task, sat in a chair facing them.

"I've said most of it already, Mother. We try to present the finest entertainment on my show. A family program. And when I heard those songs of hers, I knew this was something I wanted."

"In *short*, Mr. Sullivan . . . you like her album . . . along with the rest of those letter-writers." Sister Cluny gestured sternly toward the sacks of mail.

Sullivan was unaware that Sister Cluny was repeating what had become for her a standard phrase. He nodded.

"That's why I want her on my show! That letter the Cardinal was kind enough to send assures you of respect and dignity as far as the appearance is concerned . . . I'll shoot it anywhere and anyway you like."

"Mr. Sullivan . . . Sister Ann's music can be heard on her record." Sister Claire was aware of television: she was not aware of its incredible impact on the modern world of communications.

"But they want to see her, too, Mother."

"Why should they?"

"To see for themselves that a nun is a happy woman . . . loving other human beings, and not some . . . dried up old nut in a shell." He smiled at them shrewdly. "Isn't that why you showed me around Samaritan House before we started talking?"

"If you hadn't told me otherwise," Sister Claire smiled back, "I'd be convinced you'd been coached by Father Clementi." She turned to Sister Cluny for advice. "What do you think, Sister?"

Sister Cluny was favorably impressed. She knew a fellow businessman when she saw one. "Well, Mother . . . in view of the Cardinal's enthusiasm . . ."

"I agree." Sister Claire could save words, too. "Now as you know, Mr. Sullivan, we have a special place in our hearts for the African missions . . ."

"Yes Mother." Sullivan recognized the beginning of negotiations. "I'm sure we can arrange a contribution to the missions in lieu of the usual performance fee."

"Thank you, Mr. Sullivan. But I do have something specific in mind."

Sullivan began to worry. In the back of his brain a warning signal clanged. He seldom had been forced to beg. Perhaps these nuns were shrewder than he thought.

"Mother, I must explain that we have a top price. It's a hard and fast rule, otherwise the fees would creep up and up, until we couldn't afford anyone, anymore." He bore down hard on the feeling of tradition, giving the impression that the fee structure for his program disappeared back into antiquity, and that the ramparts of his top price had been stoutly defended by generations of Sullivans.

"Well, Mr. Sullivan, if you could see your way clear to afford . . ." she hesitated as if the sum she was about to designate would tumble from her tongue with difficulty.

"Anything within reason, Mother . . ." Sullivan quickly interjected.

"A jeep?" she managed.

"A jeep!"

Sister Claire was afraid she had gone too far; but she was determined to hold the initiative. "Could you have one delivered to the missions . . . whenever we reopen them?"

"Mother," Sullivan smiled a mixture of relief and genuine fondness, "I have to confess. I came prepared to offer quite a bit more than the price of a jeep!"

"Then you'll send one?"

Sullivan had a reputation for honesty and integrity. "A jeep can't run more than . . . what? Fifteen hundred? Two thousand dollars? I'm willing to pay ten thousand!"

The Prioress sat still for a moment, then she answered quietly. "The jeep will be all, thank you."

"But Mother . . . why don't I send the entire ten thousand?"

"Because Sister Ann will not be doing this for money; she will be doing it so that people can see that a nun is not a 'dried up old nut in a shell,' Mr. Sullivan!"

Sister Claire stood. The two of them appraised each other and liked what they had found. Mr. Sullivan extended his hand.

"You drive a hard bargain, Mother Prioress."

It hardly seemed possible that so much could be done in so short a time. A technical crew surveyed Samaritan House with such thoroughness that when the day of broadcast finally arrived they moved an armada of equipment and an army of personnel into Samaritan House at 5 A.M. and by 3 P.M. were ready to record her performance.

One week later Robert Gerarde and Mr. Duvries sat facing a large television set in the executive offices of Primavera Records. Their excitement was both professional, because of the boost the TV appearance would give the sales of her records, and personal because they wanted to see the little nun, of whom they had become so fond, come to life on that screen. One of the other executives fiddled with the dials to improve the picture, just as the image settled down and a voice unbetrayed by a thousand repetitions announced with great excitement:

"From New York . . . The Ed Sullivan Show!"

Sullivan appeared in his customary manner before the stage curtains. His head and shoulders filled the screen.

"Ladies and gentlemen, tonight we have a very special show for you. Part of it comes all the way from Belgium and a little convent in the middle of nowhere called Samaritan House."

All of the group watching in that executive office was excited. One of them mumbled something about Sister Ann being on first. Should have saved her for last, he felt.

"Shhh!" Duvries gave him a stern look devoting his full attention to Mr. Sullivan.

"You all know the Singing Nun and her records, but tonight, on our show, you will meet Sister Ann in person. Wait until you see this little nun. When we went over there to record her on video tape we had to get a special high angle to make sure we could see her over the top of her guitar!" He paused: what is known in the trade as a dramatic pause. "And now, ladies and gentlemen, the Singing Nun herself, Sister Ann."

The TV image became Sister Ann seated on a small stool in the recreation room at Samaritan House. Sister Mary and Sister Michele were beside her as she began to play and sing.

Around the world Mr. Duvries' concentration was imitated by millions. A bare foot in a *zori*, tapped in tempo against the straw mat on the floor: A Japanese businessman was being served tea by his wife in their modest home. Both enjoyed the song.

Against a wood floor a German factory worker thumped his heavy work boot while his *frau* came from washing dishes in the kitchen to listen, too.

In an over-crowded little apartment in Naples a young girl and boy sat on a couch watching their TV set. The girl looked lovingly at the boy, she leaned over, put her hand on the back of his head and kissed his cheek. He never looked away from the TV set.

Duvries sat enthralled. Despite his cynical protests he did enjoy music.

"Well, Gerarde, it's a good thing you listened to me. Might never had this girl under contract if it wasn't for me. Had to beg you to even test her, remember?"

Robert was giving him a sickly look. "But I said the good will alone was worth it, even if she were only half as good as I thought she was!" Duvries nudged the young man beside him. "Remember, Gerarde?"

"I remember, Mr. Duvries: . . . but that's not *what* I remember!" Robert was growing angry. "You didn't even want . . ."

"Easy, easy, Robert. Can't you feel your own leg being pulled?"

Robert had been so intent on the performance, so eagerly awaiting reactions, that his sense of humor had deserted him. Now he smiled.

"You'd better learn, Gerarde. I can't have a Vice-President of my own company getting sore and quitting on me, can I?" Duvries offered his hand. "Congratulations, Robert."

"Thank you, Mr. Duvries. Thank you."

"Thank her. She's wonderful! . . . And she sure sells records."

It was true: but it was an understatement compared to the impact on the record market which Sister Ann's records were about to have. Across America, in England, Canada, throughout Europe and especially in Samaritan House that evening, the whole world became fans of a woman who, until this moment, had been a voice which had pleased them from the grooves of a record. As of that night . . . The Singing Nun was a star.

Stars can be lost in their galaxies: Sister Ann was lost in a maelstrom of activities both at Samaritan House and for Primavera Records. The one thing Mother Prioress insisted upon was that there would be no further public appearances. Robert Gerarde was a respecter of protocol, but he also knew that to lift this edict required not only a special occasion but a special approach. He called Father Clementi.

Stalls in the open air market displayed fruit, vegetables, fish and the tempers of their owners. The sights and smells would have driven both a poet and a gourmet to ecstasies. Robert and Father Clementi satisfied themselves with nods of approval as they met and strolled through the heavy crowds. They paused at a cheese counter. There were wheels and blocks and squares and undefinable shapes on the counter, hanging from above, piled on shelves behind, and in the hands of a vendor. Robert sniffed the strong aroma of a small Gouda and pointed it out to the vendor.

". . . And about half a pound of well ripened Roquefort." He turned to his companion. "What about you Father? Can I get you something?"

"Well . . . the Sisters are very fond of Muenster . . ."

"The Sisters? I'm on to you, Father. Ten of them and one of you . . ." Robert indicated the soft white cheese to the vendor. "A nice chunk of Muenster . . ." he glanced at Father. "Five pounds do it?"

"Five would do nicely . . ." Father gave his most innocent smile. "Or six . . ."

Robert scowled first at the priest, then to the vendor. He had invited Father to meet him. He knew it: Father Clementi knew it. He shrugged.

"Six."

"Thank you very much, Robert."

"You just caught me in a good mood." Robert took a letter from his pocket. "I want you to see this. It's a request for Sister Ann to appear at . . ."

The priest held up his hand in mock warning. "Wait, Robert! A little Muenster only goes so far!" They laughed; each enjoying the skill with which the other skirmished. The priest became serious. "The Sisters have turned down . . . I don't know how many requests since that Sullivan show."

"Twenty-seven from me."

"Why should they suddenly say yes?"

"This one is very special: listen." He read from the opened letter in his hands:

"'Dear Mr. Gerarde: We are here at St. Joseph Orphanage. We are having a fair. Couldn't you send us the Singing Nun? She is the only one on Primavera Records we like' . . . flatterer . . . 'Yours, hopefully' . . . looks like John Joseph something . . . 'P.S. We are not asking anybody else so she *better* come!'"

"I'll convince the Sisters." Father Clementi recognized a con man from whom both he and Robert Gerarde could take lessons. "I'd better convince them: if Sister Ann doesn't come that 'John Joseph something' will write a threatening letter to the Cardinal!"

He did convince them.

Sister Ann held the large cardboard box and Sister Michele carefully tilted the last tray of fresh baked cookies into it. This was not "homework" from her nutrition class but the loving contribution to the fair at St. Joseph's Orphanage from Sister Michele and Sister Cluny. Sister Elise made a bow out of ribbon to put around the box.

"Get in there, you!" Sister Michele pushed the last cookie clinging to the tray with an adhesive of sugar.

"Watch those little imps at St. Joseph's." Sister Cluny warned. "They'll eat themselves sick if you let them."

Sister Mary was dressed for the outdoors like Sister Ann. "They'll be too busy having fun to notice if they're sick or not." Before they could close the cover and get the bow into place, the Prioress entered, crossing hurriedly to the table, followed by the remaining nuns at Samaritan House. Immediately, they were all alert, knowing that one hundred percent attendance at a hastily called meeting guaranteed something worthy of Mother Prioress' attention and theirs.

"Over here, please . . . I have some news." Sister Claire gestured them around her. They had seldom seen her so excited.

"I want to be certain we all hear this together. I just had a telephone call from Mother Superior." She looked them over, eyes alive with anticipation. They exchanged startled glances. "First, she wished me to tell all of you that she is very pleased with our progress here." Mother Prioress paused relishing her good news. "And second, to tell you that permission has just been given for our Order to re-open the Missions in Africa."

There was an instant of silence followed by a cheer. The nuns excitedly chattered their excitement: "Are we going?" "When?" "How soon!" "What about Samaritan House?" "I can't believe it!"

Sister Mary, bursting with joy, sought out Sister Ann with her eyes. The young nun stood with the box of cookies still in her arms, the only one not swept up immediately in the excited mood. As Sister Mary watched she saw Sister Ann force a smile. But it was not spontaneous: she was reacting as she knew she should. The Prioress hushed them.

"That's all I know. Mother Superior only said it would be soon . . . and I'm sure some of us will be included." She turned to Sister Ann and Sister Mary indicating their cloaks. "You have a little inspiration for the fair, don't you Sisters?"

"Yes, Mother," Sister Ann smiled.

Sister Mary noticed her watch. "We'd better go."

Sister Ann turned from the group still excitedly chattering, thrilled with their news, and reached for her guitar leaning against the wall. Her hand froze a moment on the case and her brain raced, attempting to digest the information and weigh her own feelings about it.

Africa! Six months ago . . . six weeks ago . . . she would have been the most excited nun there. Why did she feel a let down now?

CHAPTER XI

St. Joseph gave them inspiration; the weatherman provided a crisp bright day; generosity gave them a crowd. The fair was on the grounds of the rural orphanage itself, an old estate, no longer elegant but roomy and with ample grounds. The fair was improvised each year: amusement rides rented for the occasion; booths with displays and games and food; an open space with a small platform decorated with ribbons and some flowers that would be a stage. It was an annual, small, charitable event. A few hundred were in attendance, many children, over three dozen of them from the orphanage. The latter were distinguished by their drab uniform from those children who had been brought by parents to play, to provide generous support, and to see with their own eyes how fortunate were their own circumstances.

It was mid-afternoon and the entire crowd was gathered about that stage on which Sister Ann performed. Experience had honed the rough edges; and this kind of crowd was a more natural environment to her than any publicity party. She felt right at home.

. "Now this song, boys and girls, is for you. Will you help me with it?"

The children, many gathered directly in front of her, chorused a loud: "Yes, Sister!"

"Good! Sing with me then." She leaned forward toward them, "And do exactly what the song tells you to, all right?" She straightened up and began with a big full chord.

She sang a rousing folk song: "Brother John" . . . with a smile, then a frown, a tear upon his face, . . . and the children she sang to made appropriate faces imitating her with the enthusiasm and dedication and skill that only children can bring to such a song. The theme was the joining of all the human race in one big family of God. The entire crowd was with her. The children adored her. And on the fringes of that assembly, Robert Gerarde watched with more than professional interest.

It was a happy day, the highlight of the year for the orphans, and a day which the crowd had set aside for relaxation and enjoyment. Perhaps that was why none of them except Robert Gerarde noticed the strain of her performance. He could see, not the jubilant girl he knew, but a woman giving a performance good enough to convince the crowd but not someone who knew her well.

Of course, she had not told him of the Prioress' "good news".

Down the street that ran along the side of Samaritan House, Nicole Arlien raced breathlessly. She turned the corner leaped the two steps in front of the quiet convent, and knocked. She was terribly distressed. Her face was streaked with tears. She banged repeatedly on the door, clutching a man's cap in both hands.

"Answer! Answer!" she pleaded to herself. Then she remembered the bell pull and yanked it hard. It brought results in the person of the Prioress herself.

"Good afternoon . . ."

Nicole looked past her. "Where's Sister Ann?"

"She's at St. Joseph Orphanage. Singing at their little fair."

"Singing!" Nicole's grip on the cap became so tight she almost tore the visor from the cloth. "The only time you need her she's . . ." she turned away. "Forget it."

"Wait." The Prioress stopped her. "What is it you want?"

Nicole eyed her suspiciously; but her need was great. "Someone to stay with my brother . . . he's so upset! . . ."

"I can come." The Prioress' commitment was immediate and gentle.

"He'd be afraid of you. Sister Ann . . . she brought him candy and sang songs to him . . ." She attempted to suppress a sob; unsuccessfully.

"I'll come now, and leave a message for Sister to come as soon as she returns." Sister Claire had an air of authority. She recognized a cry for help when she heard one. But that very tone of authority built a barrier between herself and a suspicious young girl. All Nicole's hostility, all her fear, all her natural distrust warned her against such willingness to help.

"No!" she broke away. "We don't need any of you! I'll keep him with me!"

She raced down the street. The Prioress started to follow but within a few steps realized she could not keep up. "Wait . . . please wait . . ."

The older nun halted, watching helplessly as the footsteps echoed in the empty streets. In the middle of her jubilation of the news about Africa, in the midst of her satisfaction over the approval of Mother Superior, she suddenly appreciated and knew Sister Ann's feeling of failure.

The afternoon had spun its gossamer web of amusement over the happy throng at the fair. Evening brought shadows, a cool breeze and sleepy children. Older boys and girls ran about; the booths drew newcomers with their siren calls of fun; the noise of the crowd vied with the carousel "oom-pa-pa-". The music from one of Sister Ann's records over the public address system floated over all.

In a corner of the grounds Sister Ann rested on a garden bench. A little girl, her orphanage uniform smeared with ice cream that had dripped from a cone, was fast asleep. Her head lay in Sister Ann's lap, rumpled and grimy from the day's fun; her small legs protruded onto the bench beside Sister. The young nun, weighing her thoughts and her feelings, could see Sister Mary shepherding a mob of children onto the carousel. Sister Ann looking down at the child, was unaware of Robert Gerarde's approach. He watched them a moment.

"Too much party?" he whispered, indicating the child.

"Me, too" Sister Ann nodded. "As soon as she wakes up, Sister Mary and I will have to leave."

Robert stepped directly in front of her. "You've been hard to talk to today."

"Today is for fun," she smiled back, "Not talking."

"You know what I mean. Even when we did have a moment to talk . . . we didn't *talk*."

"About what?"

"You. Your music. Your talent. We used to argue at school over the use an artist makes of his own talent."

"I remember. Talent is a gift. We're responsible for developing whatever gifts we have . . ."

"But you're squandering yours!" Robert was insistent. He continued to whisper, respecting the child's slumber, but he wanted to be blunt. Elliptical phrases were fine for negotiating sessions; with a woman who meant as much to him as Sister Ann did he could take no chance that his meaning would not be clear. "You're wasting your life on that wretched neighborhood."

"Not a neighborhood, Robert . . . people."

"Do they understand music? Do they even understand what you're trying to do for them?"

"I don't know." Robert had touched an exposed nerve. "But does it matter?"

"It should. I don't know what you're like as a nun. I have no way of knowing that. But are you such a good one, such a terrific nun, that your musical talent isn't important any more?"

Sister Ann reacted sharply. She turned away from him hiding her own self doubt; hoping to obscure her feelings. Robert misunderstood, fearing he had offended her.

"Sorry . . . that was out of line. Sorry, Sister."

She turned back to him. "You never were the kind to beat around the bush, Robert. You might as well say all that's on your mind."

He sat on the bench, the two of them separated by the body and legs of the little orphan girl.

"The Executive Board at Primavera voted unanimously to back a world tour. For you."

"A what?" Sister's voice was loud, so surprised by the words that she forgot to whisper. She stared at him, then remembering the child's presence she lowered her voice. "That's . . . it's ridiculous. And impossible."

Robert took a telegram from his pocket and held it before her. "The start of our itinerary: concerts in New York, London, Rome . . ."

"You're dreaming . . ."

Robert would not be stopped. "When we return, you have a choice of fellowships to develop your music at the University of Louvain or Paris. You can begin the tour next month."

"I may not even *be* here next month!" It slipped out. Sister Ann regretted it before the words were completely formed, but they might as well play with all the cards, not blindly.

"I knew something was wrong with you today." He leaned forward. "I knew it! What do you mean you may not be here?"

She tried to be matter of fact. "Mother Prioress told us today the African Missions are being reopened."

"Africa!"

"I may be sent." Sister Ann kept all emotion from her voice. "I don't know."

"They can't do that to you!"

"We all volunteered when we first came to Samaritan House. I have a job to do, Robert . . . I'm still a nun."

"All right, you had this, this wonderful dedication. You tried it. Now you have a chance for something else. Something exciting and important . . . haven't you ever stopped to wonder if this . . ." he touched the sleeve of her habit ". . . is the only way for you to live?"

Sister Ann retained her wry sense of humor. "Constantly! . . . but a vocation isn't a whim. It may seem . . . I don't know what . . . strange perhaps to you. But it fills my whole life."

"Maybe then; not now!" He surveyed her for a long moment; she didn't reply. "I wanted to be sure. After today, I am sure."

"Of what?" She was off balance. "I didn't realize you were reading anything into a day . . . a simple outing with some orphans . . ."

She was not entirely convincing. And he recognized that.

"Look at yourself . . . you're a warm hearted, intelligent, talented . . . a very attractive . . ."

"A nun!" She could not let him continue.

"A very attractive young woman. In these past months . . . all the joy, all the zest in being alive that I haven't felt in years . . . it's all come back. Because of you!"

She rose abruptly lifting the child in her arms; the girl mumbled but slept on. "I can't listen, and I won't." Sister Ann was firm.

Robert stepped in front of her blocking her way. With a sleeping child in her arms she could not escape. "You can't go to Africa." He had said it. There was direct confrontation between them. "I apologize in advance. But hear me out. You put everything you can do at Samaritan House on one side of the scale . . ." He illustrated with hands extended palms up like balance pans, "Now you add the satisfaction of touching the lives of some men and women . . . and *other* women's children . . . then finally a future built out of mud huts in Africa. You weigh all of that on one side, Sister. If that's what you *really* want . . . just tell me. But on the other side you put exploring your musical gifts, the recognition your talent deserves . . . honest satisfaction in reaching people through your music. And finally . . . finally, add me." He had said even more than he intended. "By tomorrow, decide what you want."

Robert started to walk away, knowing that he had gone too far, said too much; but also knowing that if he had said less the unspoken words would thunder down on his consciousness ever afterward like rain on a tin roof.

"Robert!" she stopped him.

"*Think*, Sister Ann . . . Lucienne. Think before you find yourself tucked away on some rubbish heap of the world. Just another nun . . . and a very unhappy woman!" He had to leave. "Ten o'clock tomorrow we have a meeting at Primavera. I'll be waiting for some answers."

He hurried off. The nun was overwhelmed and deeply troubled. She could have said nothing even if he had stayed. She looked down at the child in her arms, rocking her gently. The little girl opened her eyes.

"Sister . . ." she was only half awake.

"Yes . . . what is it dear?" She forced her attention here where it was summoned.

"My stomach, Sister; I hurt . . ."

It seemed so petty a thing, especially when she was so preoccupied, that Sister Ann started to frown. But how foolish; she realized it was absurd to transfer her own troubles to the trusting little girl in her arms. She smiled.

"I hurt, too," she confided.

The ride back to Samaritan House was quiet. In the darkness Sister Mary respected her companion's need to think, suspecting its cause. The Prioress was waiting for them in the entry hall. Unaware of the strain in Sister Ann she immediately told them of Nicole's visit.

"I offered to go myself but she refused. She's terribly bitter."

Sister Ann tried to concentrate. She knew it was important; she knew she had to throw off the thoughts of herself and weigh Nicole's visit, "For the first time she came to *me*."

"If she came once," Sister Mary tried to assure her, "She'll come again."

"But I wasn't here . . ." Sister Ann knew that she could not wait for Nicole to come again.

CHAPTER XII

Nicole stood stiffly beside Dom; the two against a hostile world. The boy made no attempt to hide his tears: Nicole was coldly controlled.

"He was dead by the time I brought Dom to the hospital. The doctor said there was nothing they could do."

"No! Dear Lord, no!" She was stunned. ". . . I'm sorry . . ."

"He fell off a loading dock, trying to *prove* he could still work." Her next words were an accusation. "He was in no condition to try anything like that. The men who pulled him out of the machinery told me he was sober; and I believe them." She busied herself at the kitchen table, deliberately shutting Sister Ann out. Nicole was under such tense self-control she seemed ready to crack if anyone so much as touched her. The single small light of hope in their world was extinguished. The nun took the little boy's hand.

"Listen to me a minute, Dominic . . ."

"You can't do anything." He was all cried out.

"We can pray for him."

"Pray?" Nicole's tone was matter of fact. "You can go to hell, Sister."

The single bare bulb in the Arlien kitchen flickered in the darkened room.

"Nicole . . . if you don't want to pray, let me share your grief. It doesn't take the pain away, I know, but you can lean on me a little . . . you need all the friendship anyone can give you."

"We don't need yours." Nicole laid out the words as a mason sets bricks; row by row, building a wall meant to stand. This was not a rebuke: it was cold rejection, more stinging because it was said unemotionally.

"My father told you to stay away from us once. Now I'm telling you. Can you understand me, Sister? We don't need you, we don't want you around!"

Sister Ann looked at the two of them, nodded her head once, and turned for the door. She left them as she had found them, alone.

The darkness of the street was welcome. The nun walked briskly along, head down, toward the shelter of Samaritan House. She could not help thinking of that small glass ball which Dominic used to signal his sister. She seemed imprisoned in an artificial world that had suddenly been turned topsy turvy. Unforseen problems and mind-numbing decisions drifted down over her in a blanket which obscured the familiar landmarks of her life as the snow blotted out that miniature landscape. Not since the time in childhood when her father had died did she seem so robbed of security, floating in a world of indecision and doubt. She could think no further than the need to get home; like a wounded animal, instinct led her where she knew there was succor, both human and spiritual.

She reached the corner. From the side street, music ran down to assault her ears. The music was blaring in the quiet night; her music. It drew her. Part way down the block was a cheap record shop; the sound of her music brightened the drab surroundings more than the light pouring out of its windows onto a knot of dancing teenagers. Her path was along the main street, but she was pulled toward the music and the dancing.

The boys and girls were having a good time, humming or singing with the record. She walked to the shadows at the perimeter of the group and watched. Her own voice in the rhythmic, familiar melody of "Dominique" bounced pleasantly against her ears. In the brightly lit store windows her albums, bearing a fine pencil sketch of her, were prominently displayed.

The gay, up-tempo rhythm played against her mood, striking her anew with the contrast between her failure with Nicole and the lure of the world Robert had painted. The sound seemed to grow in intensity beating against her emotions. People were enjoying *her* music; listening to it and to what it said. Was this the world where she truly belonged?

With the melody of another of her songs trailing her down the street Sister Ann started home, moving slowly through the puddles of light from street lamps. Where was her place? Speaking to the people in her songs? . . . Or serving them in their homes? The decision closed in on her and engulfed all her thoughts and feelings like the night. She needed help.

It was very late; no traffic or pedestrians; there was just enough light from the distant street lamp to see. It gave the street on which the rectory fronted a brooding atmosphere. She was greatly disturbed but seeing the darkened building started to turn away. Before taking two steps she was back and ringing the bell. Father Clementi would understand.

She stepped back out of the shadows of the building, looking up at the second story window. Within a moment the curtain was parted spilling light from the room out onto the street. Father Clementi's face appeared squinting down to the street below. He leaned forward to see the young figure in white robes waiting for him.

"Give me a moment, Sister." He ducked back inside.

The reception room to which Father brought her bore the stamp of a man who had lived in one place for many years and expected to continue. The priest wore bedroom slippers, old pants, a worn sport shirt, open at the neck. A large patch carefully sewn over a worn spot in the back of the shirt, which no one saw when covered by his priest's garb, attested to his frugal way of life. He listened to her pour out her troubles to him with patient sympathy.

"Help me, Father. Please. I've prayed . . . I keep thinking God deserves better of me . . . but I don't know what! Or how."

"Answers . . . answers . . ." The priest searched among the clutter of his desk until he found an old tobacco humidor. He offered it to her. "Help yourself, Sister."

The matter of fact offer after an impassioned detail of trouble helped to calm the nun. She responded automatically. "I don't smoke, Father."

Father Clementi looked down at the humidor and smiled. "It's chocolate. The doctor made me quit two years ago."

She declined with a shake of her head.

"A substitute, chocolate . . . but not the real thing, Sister. And you don't want substitutes for real answers." He needed time to think; took a piece of the chocolate and sucked on it.

"I've been here ten years. A lot of people have asked me hard questions. The one thing I've learned, Sister, is that answers, real answers, usually come from the people who asked the questions in the first place." He stared at her for a long moment. Then asked bluntly, "Do you want to leave the convent?"

Sister Ann looked at him for a long moment, jolted by his directness. It was a question she had not anticipated; a question she had not asked herself. But Father Clementi had seized upon the real choice. He was a strong man, Father Clementi. He had to be to endure the sadness all around him for all these years, yet not become softened by an overdose of pity nor hardened by the daily repetition of misery. He waited patiently for her answer.

"I've spent five years getting here, Father. I joined . . . because I wanted to serve Our Lord, through men. But all I've succeeded in doing is . . . disturb Robert. And giving myself a lot of anguish."

Father Clementi was too wise to allow self pity to cloy difficult choices. "Because you've spent five years becoming a nun is a very poor reason for staying one."

Sister Ann agreed. "I want to do something really worthwhile with my life. I can feel that in a song . . . why not when it's time to *act?*"

Father Clementi nodded. He was beginning to understand the depth of her dilemma. "Sister, I never met anyone who didn't want to live a worthwhile life. Or at least didn't say he wanted to. The question is never, do we want to live worthwhile lives, but do we love God enough to do something about it? In your case, and mine, it means giving nothing less than our entire lives."

"But isn't the music worthwhile, too?"

"Agreed. So is being a wife and mother. So is working hard at any labor. So is being an artist. So are a lot of things 'worthwhile', Sister. You have to decide: Robert and the tour and all they have to offer . . . or all the Nicole Arliens you'll meet as a nun for the rest of your life."

"That's a hard choice!"

"Isn't that why you came here? To make that choice?"

"I guess I really came to try to avoid making it, myself."

"Sacrifice means giving, to a point where it hurts, and then some. No strings attached. If you've done your job as a nun because you expect appreciation and thanks . . . then you're not acting out of spiritual motives, Sister. You chose to be a nun. Perhaps this is the first time you're coming face to face with what that really means: a woman making a gift of herself to others, because she feels that every man, woman and child is her spiritual brother. Giving that big a gift is very difficult. Can you do it, joyfully, because you love Our Lord? When you can . . . you'll know what kind of vocation you really have."

They were hard words but they were the right ones. Sister Ann paused a long moment before she answered, very softly. "What if I can't, Father?"

"It's *your* choice." Until this moment the priest had been firm allowing no emotion or pity to blur an understanding of choice he had tried to make clear for her. But now his face filled with compassion. "I'll pray that either way, Sister . . . you choose well."

Sister Ann reached the door of Samaritan House fumbled in the darkness to insert the key in the lock, opened it and entered quietly. A light burned in the hall. Sitting in a chair by the entrance was Sister Mary, fast asleep, head slumped on her shoulder. When Sister Ann saw her she understood immediately that her friend had kept a vigil, wanting to help if she could when Sister Ann returned. Her presence there did help.

The nuns seldom gave expression to the affection among them. The comfort of praying together daily in the chapel; of singing the mass together; of receiving the Holy Eucharist together; of working side by side in the kitchen and in the yard; these were the bonds of deep, loving care that tied one member of this family of nuns to the others in enduring if unstated permanence.

Sister Ann gently tapped the African nun's shoulder, waking her. Sister Mary opened her eyes, suppressing a yawn. "I guess I fell asleep . . ." She smiled realizing the obviousness of what she had said. Then she rose, pushed her chair back. She looked at Sister Ann knowing questions were out of place. And, between them, unnecessary.

"Thanks for waiting up, Sister."

"I slept as well in the chair as I would have upstairs, I think." She started up the stairs pausing for Sister Ann to follow.

"I can't sleep yet."

"Want to talk it over?"

"Thanks . . . I, I don't think talk can help me."

There was a moment of understanding between them. Sister Mary reached out and touched her fellow nun's cheek with her fingertips; a gesture of care for her. Then she started up the stairs.

Sister Ann was struck suddenly with the foolishness of prejudice. She felt love through those gentle fingertips; and love has no color. She called softly after her, "Goodnight."

"Goodnight," Sister Mary returned.

She watched her friend disappear, then walked slowly to the chapel. The only light came from a vigil lamp burning at the altar. She walked slowly down the short aisle to the front of the chapel. She knelt. Above her the crucifix stood out against the whitewashed wall; shadows flickered over the corpus. She began to sing to herself, very softly, very slowly . . . a form of praying that was most profound for her since childhood.

Her voice faded away. There was torture on her face and anguish. Then she bowed her head very low, sinking down almost in physical pain, wanting to express in physical gesture the prayer that in her, "Thy will be done."

CHAPTER XIII

The guitar rested on a table in the entry hall, waiting: alongside it was a copy of Sister Ann's album. By nine o'clock in the morning all of the nuns had long since attended Mass, completed breakfast and the domestic tasks necessary to begin a morning and embarked upon their day. Sister Therese had drawn this day as her turn to do the cleaning. She was not the kind to sweep around things. She moved the table, swept the floor carefully, then replaced it against the wall, straightening the items with care which had been left on it. The album attracted her attention. She surveyed the cover critically, then smiled her satisfaction and began humming "Dominique" as she continued working.

Sister Mary walked past her toward the recreation room. She carried a small pot with a home grown tropical orchid newly in blossom. She had a triumphant smile. Sister Therese was so astonished that the broom flew from her fingers.

"Ooooh! Beautiful, Sister! How did you get that to grow here?"

Sister Mary grinned. "Hid it behind the stove! Opened this morning."

Sister Therese followed her into the recreation room. Both of them were so interested in the magnificent blossom they almost stumbled over Sister Elise who was backing toward the door unwinding an enormous skein of tangled knitting yarn. She caught sight of Sister Therese and clutched her arm.

"Another victim! Stand right here."

Sister Therese stared at her blankly. At the far end of the recreation room, holding the other end of the yarn looped over two outstretched hands, was Sister Michele. Sister Elise moved to a chair which she had used as the second terminus for her enormous loop of yarn. She lifted this end of the loop, dumped it over Sister Therese's now outstretched arms. Sister Mary set her orchid in a place of honor near the window. She watched the activity of the other nuns curiously.

"What are you going to make? A sweater for an elephant?"

Sister Elise was creating an enormous ball of yarn, winding as she unravelled it from the huge loop which the other two sisters now held for her. She assumed an injured air. "I got this free because it was twisted. You can't teach knitting without yarn, Sister!"

The doorbell rang before Sister Mary could return the jibe. She hurried to answer it.

A plainly dressed plump man stood there, with the patient air of an official.

"Sister Ann?"

"No. But she's here." Sister Mary gestured him in and noted Sister Ann coming down the stairs from her room. "This gentleman wants to see you, Sister," she called.

Sister Ann carried her cloak. She identified herself and waited for the man to respond. From his inside pocket he pulled a wallet, opening it to display an identification card.

"I'm from the Welfare Service, Sister. Do you know the Arlien children?"

"Yes." Sister Ann reacted suddenly. "What happened?"

"I came to take them to their father's funeral . . . they're gone!"

"You looked everywhere?" She was genuinely alarmed.

He nodded. "Do you know anything, Sister? Any place they might be?"

Sister Ann hesitated, concentrating her thoughts on the problem at hand. "I can't tell you," she finally stated.

"Sister, kids around here think I'm some kind of . . . dog catcher for humans. You know better."

The man was right. Sister Ann checked her watch. "I'll go myself." She looked at him seeking understanding. "Your word; you won't follow me to where I look for them?"

The man appriased her. "My word."

"Please drive me to their house." She started for the door.

"Your appointment, Sister," Sister Mary called after her. "Robert Gerarde?"

"When he comes, ask him . . . to wait for me at the Arlien house."

She was about to leave when she remembered the guitar and came back for it. Sister Mary held the guitar out to her. The two nuns looked into each other's faces. The guitar and meeting Robert represented a choice; the African nun sensed that Sister Ann's accepting it and of her appointment were not routine.

Finally Sister Ann took the guitar.

"Goodby, Sister . . ." Sister Mary spoke for her alone.

The young nun could not return her steady look. She waved goodby and hurried out after the social worker. Sister Mary watched her climb into his car and speed off down the street.

Dominic held the glass ball upright in his hand. He

turned it over; the snow fell. On the bench along the far wall of their hideout Nicole sat playing a mournful tune on her harmonica. Beside them was a bulging battered suitcase, a large handbag of Nicole's, and their coats. They had begun at first light; packing their few possessions, making certain they had left nothing important in the apartment, buying what little food they could afford. It didn't take long.

The two of them had begun their long vigil in the secret place, waiting for nightfall and the chance to escape. Dom, sobered by his father's death and by the seriousness of their situation, held the small glass toy out to his sister.

"Could I take this?" She stopped playing the harmonica and slid to the floor beside him.

"Sure, Dom. We'll make room."

"Where will we go?"

Nicole assumed a cheerful air. "Far away from here . . . maybe we'll move around for a while . . ." She smiled for his benefit. ". . . like tourists!"

"On a train?" He was intrigued.

"Maybe . . . I don't know yet. I'll have to make some money. Then we'll decide where we want to go." The girl leaned over to him and hugged the small boy close. "Just the two of us."

"I'll do just what you tell me, Nicole."

"Good boy." She held him away for a moment; he was not only her brother and her responsibility but a trusting little child who depended on her. "Now you better take a nap, Dom. As soon as it's dark we leave."

He nodded agreement, leaned over and kissed her cheek. She returned it, then helped him settle down to rest his head against her shoulder. But when he could no longer see, her face dropped the cheerful mask and showed the worry she was concealing.

Sister Ann instructed the social worker to park his car on a side street. He agreed to stay there. She turned the corner, found the alley beside the Arlien home, walked along it into the deserted yard. At this hour of the morning there was a surprising glare from the sun. She got her bearings and started across to the secret entrance to the warehouse.

Dom slept. His small face was relaxed, his eyes closed restfully. Nicole still supported him against her shoulder. Suddenly, hearing a noise below she became wary.

"Dom . . ." she whispered.

The boy raised himself, starting to ask her a question; but she covered his mouth with her hands. They must not be discovered.

Sister Ann climbed the stairs, dread resting heavily in the pit of her stomach. When she reached the top she saw them. None of them spoke for a moment. Sister Ann entered the room, her eyes taking in the suitcase, the bag, the obvious preparations for flight.

"Back again?" Nicole was wary. She did not know how much the nun might know.

Sister Ann came to the point. "The man from the Welfare Service is looking for you. . . ."

"You told *him* where we . . ."

"I didn't tell him anything," Sister Ann interrupted. "I came alone." Wakened from his nap the little boy's head was still filled with the dreams Nicole had helped design for him. He was pleased to see the nun.

"We're going away, Sister," he confided, full of anticipation. "We're going to ride on trains and go any place we want!"

Nicole reproached him sharply. Instinctively she knew that this nun represented a threat to their security. Through all her life adults, figures in authority, the ones you were supposed to trust, had alway betrayed her hopes. The social workers were the enemy: the ones they must elude like escaping criminals. But this nun was an even greater threat . . . because she knew their secret hiding place.

"You're running away, Nicole?" Sister Ann stood directly before the girl so she could not avoid answering.

"They want to put Dominic in an orphanage."

The boy studied his sister anxiously. "You won't let them, will you, Nicole?" The word orphanage had brought to his mind a vague and grim image of a large institution with barred windows and a hoard of small children with hearts also imprisoned. It was the thing he dreaded above all others.

Nicole reassured him. "We're going to stay together, Dom. I wouldn't let anybody take you away from me."

Sister Ann, alone of the three of them, recognized how hopeless was the girl's plan. She knew that at this moment, she herself must come up with a solution. She wanted to help. She had to. "What if I got you a job? I'm sure I could. At Primavera Records. It would be a decent job, Nicole . . ."

Nicole shook her head. "They won't let me keep him. I'm not eighteen yet . . . they'll start checking and find out about those pictures."

The words stuck in her throat and gagged her mind, but all her senses were sharply tuned to the need to escape. She could see that the nun wanted to help. Maybe that desire to help was the key to freedom. She watched Sister Ann carefully. "If you really want to do something, Sister, help us get away from here!"

Sister Ann was tempted to do just that. But she too was thinking quickly. She realized that it would be defying the law, even with these children for whom she felt such sympathy. She also recognized that this was a moment in Nicole's life which might determine her future maturity. "Nicole, you can't run away . . . you have to accept the way things are . . ."

"Oh, I accept it, Sister. 'The way things are' is that nobody gives one little damn for either one of us!"

"We all have to make decisions sometimes . . . that aren't easy. You have to decide for Dom as well as yourself. Do you want to live like criminals, always running away, having to . . . to do things you don't want to . . . just to feed yourselves?"

The nun was not going to help. The tips of Nicole's

fingers grew cold and her control began to evaporate: she knew fear. "You think this is something new, Sister? It's always been the same. The only thing in this world that means anything to me now is Dom . . . so naturally Dom is what they want to take away!"

Sister Ann pleaded, "Nicole . . . Dom . . ." They had to understand. "I'll talk to people; I'll do everything I can; but even if they don't allow it right away, you'll be eighteen soon. You'll have a job. You'll prove you should have a chance to keep Dom with you."

"Papa was out of work for six years," Nicole snapped. "Whoever gave him a chance?"

Dom suddenly began to cry. The talk flowing back and forth over his head had released tears, and they came now. Big, choking, little-boy-afraid sobs. Sister Ann knelt down beside him, reaching out for him. "Dom, oh Dom . . ."

The nun was deeply moved but the little boy looked up from his tears directly in her face and shook his head violently "No." He said nothing but drew away quickly and buried his head against his sister. The rejection hurt more than any words ever could.

She stood up struggling for self-control, knowing that if she allowed herself to collapse in tears she would fail to help them and lose somehow the battle that was beginning to rage within herself.

Nicole mothered her brother tenderly. His tears cracked the tough shell she had built around herself. She hugged him fiercely and gently apologized for him. "He can't help it."

Sister Ann felt defeated, but had nothing further to offer; no plan; no genuine hope. Yet she could not betray them. "I won't say anything, Nicole. But sooner or later you'll be discovered."

"We'll get away."

"And then?"

Nicole shrugged. "Hide someplace else a few days . . ."

Sister Ann forced her to face reality. "And *then,* Nicole?"

"And then, and then!" Suddenly Nicole collapsed in tears. "So you're right, they'll find us sooner or later, they'll find us!" She turned away, almost immediately regaining control and roughly wiping away the tears which betrayed her fear and weakness.

"Sure, that's the . . . 'the way things are', isn't it, Sister? Who am I kidding?"

She knew the conclusion was inevitable. She looked long at her little brother then at Sister Ann. The stamp of defeat on her was painful to witness. It was a long moment before Sister Ann broke the silence.

"The man . . . he's waiting on the street . . ."

Nicole gently broke her brother's embrace and picked up her suitcase.

"We gonna go away? Huh, Nicole, like you said?" Dom was still hopeful.

Nicole hesitated. The trusting face watched her eagerly: she could not return the look. She concentrated her attention on the suitcase and beckoned him to his own things. Her voice was flat.

"Take your things. You're all alone and so am I. That's the way the world is, Dom . . . I can't do anything about it."

The boy looked from her to Sister Ann, at first incredulous, then totally defeated. He liked that nun. Yet somehow she must be to blame. His world, his friend, even his sister . . . they would never be the same. His shoulders sagged; he shuffled after Nicole.

At that moment, watching them, Sister Ann's heart broke.

CHAPTER XIV

The drab official car of the Welfare Service Juvenile Division was parked on the side street around the corner from the Arlien home. The welfare worker waited nervously leaning against his car and smoking. All the nun had told him was that he must wait there and not follow her. He knew the children were not in their home and he could see the evidence of their flight. Where they could be he could not even guess. He had to trust the nun.

Three teenagers strolled up surveying the car and the man. They were not toughs; but like most of the young people in this neighborhood they were hostile toward the authorities. There were few secrets on these streets. They lived in a goldfish bowl of common necessity and misery. The youths knew the Arliens; they saw Mr. Arlien frequently in the cafes and on the streets; they knew the children. All of them had heard of the father's death. And although deep expressions of sympathy were as scarce as money, what they felt in their hearts was another matter. A few adults from the neighborhood watched in resigned curiosity from a distance as the youths approached the car. One of them glanced toward the Arlien home and then at the welfare worker.

"You don't even wait until the old man's in his grave, do you?"

The man was a veteran. He knew the way their minds worked. "I feel as badly about what happened as you do," he replied gently. "I want to help those children."

The smallest of the three youths was the leader. "Help them right into a juvenile home?" He was sad, not belligerent. "Never 'help' me, will you, mister?"

They moved off as aimlessly as they had approached. Life, they knew went on.

Sister Ann led the two children each laden with a few precious possessions around the corner from the alley and toward the car. The welfare worker spotted them. He took a few steps toward them, relieved that they were safe and coming with him. Then he saw their faces and stopped. His relief that they had been found gave way for a feeling of their plight.

He turned gravely to his car and busied himself opening doors to both front and back. There was not much he could say; and his experience warned him that in cases like this the first sad moments were often the worst. Better to say nothing and avoid stirring up bitterness. He would get them in the car, drive them where they must go and their accepting their fate would grow with every passing mile. His only consolation was his conviction that what he was doing for them was in their own best interests.

Sister Ann's guitar lay crosswise on the rear seat. He removed it so that they could enter more readily and rested it against the rear fender.

The children reached the car. One glance at Sister and the man knew not to ask where they had been or how she had gotten them to come.

"I'll put these in back." He took the battered bags and the few small items of clothing and swiftly stored them in the trunk. All four stood now, awkwardly looking at the car.

"Goodbye, Dom." Sister Ann hugged him.

Dom suffered her embrace and stood waiting.

"We'll all sit together. Up front," the man instructed gently.

Dom slid into the front seat and sat glumly in the center. The man crossed quickly past Sister; seeing Nicole under such a strain he hesitated, decided not to thank the nun, and moved to the driver's side. He started the engine.

On the littered sidewalk, Nicole deliberately smoked a cigarette to a short stub, reluctant to leave; her last small gesture of independence toward a world which had overwhelmed her. Sister Ann took her guitar from where it rested against the rear fender. As Nicole bent to enter the nun suddenly blocked her.

"This is Sister Adele." She held it out between them. "I never had to give it up . . . the way you have to lose Dom." She rushed on. "You like music; if you try you can learn to play it."

Very gently she pushed the guitar into the girl's hand. She was filled with emotion. "When you feel . . . the way you feel right now, Nicole . . . all alone . . ." She flicked her fingers across the strings, a farewell caress, . . . "play this guitar and remember, . . . you're *not* alone: God loves you." She swallowed. "Remember that . . . because just to prove it . . . a foolish, struggling woman, in these funny white robes, gave up something that . . . that means a great deal."

Nicole took it in her outstretched hands, stared at the nun for a moment and then at the guitar. Tears formed in her eyes and trickled down her cheeks. She sobbed just once; then looked at the nun.

"I . . ." she pulled the guitar close against her. "Thank you." She could not control herself; instead she turned sharply and sat in the front seat, slamming the door. "Thank you . . . Sister Ann!"

The car pulled away moving slowly down the street.

Sister Ann's hands were still out in front of her where she had held the guitar. She let them slide to her sides. Suddenly she reached into her pocket and took out the guitar pick, holding it up in one hand taking a step toward the retreating car. She halted; held the pick in front of her face, in her open palm, staring at it, realizing how much she had just given away. How much.

Her hands closed around the pick, clutching hard. In the distance the car, gathering momentum, reached the end of the street. It turned the corner and disappeared.

Sister Ann's clenched hand was still in front of her. The guitar was a symbol of one part of her life in and out of the convent. Its surrender had been a declaration that being a living witness of the love of God was more important to her than any other thing. There were tears on her face now, too. Her sacrifice left her nothing; except the joy that she was able to make it. She opened the hand with the pick, deliberately cupping both hands around it; then folded the two hands together, flat palm to flat palm, in a gesture for prayer. She smiled. Around her, the street had resumed its lonely emptiness. She stood there, alone, and finally dropped her hands to her sides.

From the direction in which the welfare worker's car had disappeared, Robert Gerarde's shiny Mercedes rounded a corner and pulled up across from the Arlien house. Robert jumped out started across the street toward the house but suddenly spotted Sister Ann. He called to her.

". . . Lucienne!"

Sister Ann walked briskly away. Back to Samaritan House. Robert halted in the middle of the street. She was leaving. She didn't hear his call. The nun moved faster. With new dedication she took a big gulp of fresh air and smiled as she looked up at the buildings on the street. She was full of love and very, very happy.

CHAPTER XV

Robert Gerarde paced impatiently in a small courtyard alongside the old church. Summer was waning but the morning sun was still very warm. He ground out a cigarette with his foot as the bells in the church tower began to clang the passage of another hour. Mass must be over. The wooden side door swung open and two boys dressed as acolytes tumbled out into the yard. One carried a still smoking censer. Robert watched him find a spot of dirt to empty the smoldering charcoal. No wonder it was taking so long; it had been a High Mass. He moved to the door and, squinting at the contrasting darkness from the sunlight outside, he made out Father Clementi's figure in the sacristy. The priest, still wearing cassock and surplice, came to greet him.

"Robert!" They shook hands warmly.

"Hello, Father!"

"It's been too long, too long." Father Clementi indicated the stone steps. "Sit down; it's a little warm in there." From time to time he waved at passing parishioners on their way home from church. This was no distant priest-on-the-altar and people-in-the-pews kind of parish. They all knew that he lived there much as they lived.

Robert sat down beside him, as Father Clementi wiped his perspiring forehead with his handkerchief. "How's Samaritan House, Father?"

"Flourishing. And the record business?"

"It keeps me going round and round . . ."

Father Clementi made a face at the bad pun. They were good friends though it had been weeks since they had seen each other. He guessed it was not only business that had kept Robert from coming. Why make a man sweat to find an opening in their conversation to bring up a delicate subject?

"You want to hear about Sister Ann, don't you, Robert." The man nodded. "She's in a little bush village . . . I've forgotten the name . . . it's about forty miles from Leopoldville." Robert frowned. It was what he had heard, but as long as it was unconfirmed he could sustain the hope that this was wrong. "She's very happy, Robert. I'll show you the letter . . . the words shine on the page."

Robert found another cigarette and lit it. "I guess she made the right decision . . . and that's what's important."

"I think so."

"But it's hard to think of her . . . out in the middle of nowhere."

"Robert, she's out there . . ." Father Clementi groped for the words, "being a kind of mirror. So those people can see God's love of all mankind . . . in her. Ever look at a mirror, tilted to catch the rays of the sun and reflecting it?" He held out his hand and tilted the palm like an imagined mirror. "You can't look at it, the light is so dazzling." He looked straight at Robert. "That's the way she feels."

Robert smoked for a moment in silence. Then he

looked at the priest and smiled, glad that he had come, glad that there was a Father Clementi to come to.

"Thanks, Father . . . thanks."

"I have the letter over at the rectory."

"I don't mean to rush you, Father; but why don't you get changed so I can buy you a good meal and tell you what's new at Primavera."

The priest rose. "I seldom refuse an invitation . . . in fact I seldom get an invitation, especially to a good meal." He crossed to the door of the sacristy. "But next time, Robert . . . why don't you wait for me inside the church instead of out here?"

Robert Gerarde smiled: you had to admire a man who never stopped trying.

No photographs, no words, not even the descriptions of Sister Mary's had ever been adequate to bring to life the reality of Africa. Far from the bustling city of Leopoldville spindly trees surrounded a village on the plain, adding more decoration than shade. It was a desolate spot. The few huts were made of thatched grass and mud, one or two had corrugated roofs. Naked children ran with a few skinny dogs, but there was a listless air. It was too hot, and the adults had too little hope. A cloud of dust heralded the arrival of a battered ancient truck in this human no-man's-land between life and death. It came to a wheezing halt. A rumpled Dominican priest climbed down from the driver's seat and assisted the four young nuns from the back. Sister Ann and Sister Mary stepped down weary and hot; as the priest helped the other two they glanced about them, then at each other. What they saw was very discouraging.

"Well . . ." Sister Mary was the first to speak. "Welcome to the African Missions."

Sister Elise and Sister Michele helped the priest take down their bags. None of the villagers approached them.

"As you can see, Sisters . . . you're sorely needed here!"

"No sense in sight seeing, Father," Sister Ann gave him a wry smile. "What can we do?"

"Why don't you two see what's left of our old church." He pointed, "Down at the end of the street."

The street was a barren stretch of earth between a few huts. It was dirty and very dusty. Here and there a man or a woman sat and stared at their passage. There was neither greeting nor hostility, only apathy. Sister Ann smiled occasionally at someone, but even the children stared back with total disinterest. The two nuns didn't see a church.

"Where is the church, please?" Sister Mary asked in Swahili?

An unsmiling woman stared at them a long moment. Then pointed vaguely to a hut nearby. They turned to look at it.

Two wooden sticks in the form of a cross clung to the roof, though fallen to a rakish angle. The hut itself was fairly large for this village; lack of care had changed it for the worse. Some of the roof was missing or decayed. Dirt and refuse decorated the doorless opening. The two nuns exchanged another look.

"There's no place like home." Sister Ann indicated the doorway, "After you Sister."

The darkness inside the church was relieved by openings in the roof. The two nuns entered with their bags. Almost immediately they were startled to hear a groan. They moved cautiously toward the sound.

"Who's there? . . . Who is it?" Sister Mary's Swahili sputtered in the silence.

Sister Ann spotted something and pointed. She moved quickly to a dim side of the hut and bent down. A native woman lay on a straw pallet, emaciated and very weak. Sister Ann knelt down beside her. "What's wrong?" She beckoned to Sister Mary. "Talk to her Sister! She looks half dead!"

"No wonder." Sister Mary moved beside her carrying a naked young baby not more than 10 or 12 days old.

The woman saw it. She spoke through cracked lips, the Swahili coming in gasps and whispers. "My baby. She's hungry . . ."

Sister Mary handed the tiny infant to Sister Ann and started to open a medical kit.

"Where's her family?" Sister Ann queried her companion. "What's she doing here all alone?"

Sister Mary relayed the questions in Swahili as she found the proper tools she sought in her kit. The woman looked from one nun to the other turning only her eyes, her head too weak for even that movement. Her answer was halting. Sister Mary waited for her to finish, then interpreted softly to Sister Ann.

"She's not married. This is the only place she could find to stay . . . the village says the baby is . . . bad luck."

Sister Ann knelt beside the woman, laid the infant in her arms and began to comfort her by bathing away the perspiration with her handkerchief. She spoke to Sister Mary, but her eyes and her smile remained with the woman.

"Sister, how do I say to her: 'You're not alone anymore'?"

In less than a year Samaritan House had become a success by any standards. The recreation room became the common meeting place of the neighborhood. Most gatherings there were open to anyone who wished to come but not this one.

Father Clementi, Sister Claire and the other nuns sat in the dim room, shades drawn over the windows, as a film projector borrowed for the occasion clacked noisily throwing its beam of light on the screen at the end of the room. The film revealed a wobbly panorama of the small African village. It was followed by a large closeup of Sister Ann smiling straight at all of them. In her hand she held a microphone and from the loudspeaker in the recreation room she spoke to them.

"Hello Sister Claire, Father Clementi and all the rest of you back at Samaritan House. Isn't this sound recording system a terrific addition for our report from Africa? Please thank Mr. Gerarde for sending it out here. I hardly know where to begin . . . except to tell you that within a month we saw our first elephant, and our first vulture. Sister Claire, we all hope Mother Superior finds a replacement for you very soon so you can join us . . . all of us miss you."

The image on the screen altered from Sister Ann to shots of the village. It absorbed all of those watching in that recreation room until they felt themselves right there with their companions.

The village was still primitive and isolated yet it had a new vigor. The street was swept, the huts clean, the people alert and smiling. They showed the biggest change, the return of their self-respect. The church had a fresh coat of whitewash; its cross was straight. There was the picture of another hut, the same as those around it in the village.

"This is our convent. We built it with plenty of help. Sister Michele claims it resembles her old room at Samaritan House . . . only more comfortable."

On the screen Sister Michele and Sister Elise stepped out of the hut unaware that they were being photographed. Then in pantomime they reacted to being called from off screen and did a sequence of double takes: "You mean right now?" "Where's the camera?" "Who me?" and finally a sickly grin and wave at the camera in a time honored tradition of home movies. Then there was Sister Elise instructing a group of native women in sewing some garments made of very bright cloth. Sister Ann's voice continued.

"Sister Elise has already managed to start a sewing club. It's very hot, and her biggest difficulty was convincing the children that they should wear any clothes, no matter who made them or how pretty they are!"

On a small wooden stand at which two native men were working Sister Mary appeared on the screen. Around her in front of the hut was a horde of children, ranging from about one year to six. They were ragged but cheerful and clean. A few mothers were in the background. Sister Ann held her microphone so they could be recorded together. In the background there was plenty of yowling from the children.

"Tell them about your polio vaccine, Sister."

Sister Mary seemed embarrassed at using a microphone but she was obviously beloved by her own people in a special way. "Polio is a terrible problem here. And unfortunately some native doctors had a horrible potion that was the accepted prescription. So I read that in America they give drops of vaccine on sugar cubes. And I adapted the idea." She held up a sample. "Sugar cane! The kids beg for 'Sister's potion'!"

As she said those words the children saw her raise the sample of sugar cane and she and Sister Ann were surrounded by children until the camera held by one of the other nuns was jostled and the screen swirled as it dropped from the hands of the holder.

When the image cleared it showed Sister Ann again standing in front of the chapel. She spoke directly to her audience.

"The Sisters have all asked me to say one thing . . . from all of us. We thank you for letting us come here. And for preparing us with the new approach. I continue to learn right here. At first I missed my singing, and especially my guitar. So I began singing with the boys of the village. They taught me all over again that the essence of prayer and of song is in the depth of feeling of those who pray and sing." She smiled. "We want you to look now and see if you don't agree with us."

The last shots of the film were of Mass in progress in the chapel. The altar in the background was a crude wooden table; the priest faced his congregation and intoned . . . "Gloria in excelsis Deo . . ."

A group of boys were shown next; perhaps 40 of them standing there neatly dressed. They responded to the *Gloria;* but the response and the singing were unlike anything the audience in Samaritan House had ever seen or heard before. The boys sang liturgical music in an explosion of sound. Tom-toms beat; strange rhythmic patterns and novel melodies replaced the precise Gregorian chant. It was distinctively native in character; although the words and actions of the priest at the altar helped to make it recognizable as the same *Gloria*. This strange music from that far off land filled the room. The screen showed devout faces of Sister Michele and Sister Elise and Sister Mary; they knelt not separately, but intermingled with the men, women and children of the village.

The last moments of the film returned to that exultant choir of boys. Standing before them waving her arms and conducting them was Sister Ann. She stood on a box, in order to be seen; but as she sang lustily with them it required nothing more than her face to reveal her mood.

It was magnificently fitting; pure joy.

3-66

Here's an Outstanding Opportunity to Enhance Your Home Library

4 volumes of literary masterpieces by the World's greatest storytellers selected by Thomas B. Costain and John Beecroft. A $15 hardcover value, yours for the unbelievably low price of $2.95 if you act now.

1 Stories To Remember, vol. I

3 complete novels plus 19 stories, including THE BIRDS by Daphne du Maurier, PORTRAIT OF JENNY by Robert Nathan, THE BLUE CROSS by G. K. Chesterton.

2 Stories To Remember, vol. II

2 complete novels plus 14 stories, including THE SEA OF GRASS by Conrad Richter, THE SIRE OF MALATROIT'S DOOR by Robert Louis Stevenson, MOTHER IN MANNVILLE by Marjorie Kinnan Rawlings.

3 More Stories To Remember, vol. III

2 complete novels plus 17 stories, including OLD MAN AT THE BRIDGE by Ernest Hemingway, THE CYPRIAN CAT by Dorothy L. Sayers, LADY L. by Romain Gary, THE RETURN OF THE RANGERS by Kenneth Roberts.

4 More Stories To Remember, vol. IV

2 complete novels plus 15 stories, including BABYLON REVISITED by F. Scott Fitzgerald, TURN ABOUT by William Faulkner, THE MURDER OF ROGER ACKROYD by Agatha Christie.

Mail Coupon Right Away For All Four Books!

Popular Library, Dept. 60-8015
355 Lexington Ave.
New York, N.Y. 10017

Send me postpaid the complete set of paperback books—9 novels and 65 stories—in 4 volumes, boxed. I'm enclosing $2.95, and if not fully satisfied, I may return the books in good condition within 10 days for a full refund.

Name_____

Address_____

City_____

State_____ Zip #_____